**"You deal with identity theft in your company, don't you, Kyle?"** Lindsey asked, pressing her cell phone to her ear.

"Sure. Why?"

"It's my father. I found at least two dozen letters from collection agencies in his desk."

"Does your father have debt?"

"My father's a miser when it comes to money. I don't think he's ever had debt." She knew she shouldn't be dragging Kyle into this, but she didn't know who else to turn to. "I'm sorry to dump all this on you. I'm sure you didn't have this conversation in mind when you called."

"I was thinking of something more along the lines of asking you to dinner, actually."

Lindsey smiled. "Dinner would be nice. I—"

She was interrupted by the violent sound of shattering glass. She jumped up from the table and spun around. The metal handle on the back door shook. Someone was breaking in.

## LISA HARRIS

Currently, Lisa and her husband, along with their three children, are working in Mozambique as church planters. She speaks French and is fervently working to improve her Portuguese. Life is busy between ministry and homeschooling, but she loves her time to escape into another world and write, and sees this work as an extension of her ministry.

Besides writing, Lisa loves to travel. She and her husband have visited more than twenty countries throughout Europe, Africa, South America and the Far East, and have lived in Togo, France, South Africa, Brazil and currently Mozambique. One of her favorite pastimes is learning to cook different exotic dishes from around the world. Be sure to check out her Web site at www.lisaharriswrites.com or her blog at mybloginthheartofafrica.blogspot.com for a peek into her life in the heart of Africa.

# LISA HARRIS

# FINAL
# Deposit

Steeple
Hill ®

Published by Steeple Hill Books™

STEEPLE HILL BOOKS

Steeple
Hill®

ISBN-13: 978-0-373-44308-6
ISBN-10:     0-373-44308-0

FINAL DEPOSIT

www.SteepleHill.com

**Printed in U.S.A.**

In Him we have redemption through His blood, the forgiveness of sins, in accordance with the riches of God's grace.

—*Ephesians,* 1:7

This book is dedicated to Mema. I miss you.

## Acknowledgments

The past year has been a roller coaster of adventure, from the tropical paradise of northern South Africa to the busy rush of a Brazilian city, and now the white beaches of Mozambique. Thankfully, none of my adventures have been quite as perilous as they were for my hero and heroine. Through all these changes, I never could have kept on writing if it weren't for my wonderful and supportive husband and kids, my awesome critique group and members of my extended family, who are always there with an encouraging word when times get crazy. And believe me, it's been crazy!

Thanks also to my agent, Joyce, for always cheering me on, my editor, Krista, for believing in this story, and for Louise, who did a great job— and fairly painlessly, I might add—in helping me edit this story.

# PROLOGUE

Whoever said that love of money was the root of all evil had never experienced the financial benefits of working a long con.

Leaning against the light post outside his London flat, Abraham Omah nodded at the familiar face of a woman as she jogged past, iPod on her arm, Windbreaker zipped up to block the April chill. She smiled at him as he took a drag off his cigarette, and then flicked the ashes onto the sidewalk. She was definitely worth pursuing, but she'd have to be a prize for another day. He had more pressing things to consider at the moment.

His lips curled into a grin at the thought of George Taylor. Contact with Mr. Taylor had grown into daily online chats, e-mails and even an occasional phone call charged to the American's bill. It continued to amaze him how trusting people could be. Throw out the tempting lure of easy money and watch the gullible jump headfirst into the game.

He couldn't help but chuckle. Anyone that naive deserved what they got.

A taxi driver blared his horn as he sped down the narrow roadway congested with other cars, buses and bikers. Abraham tossed his cigarette onto the sidewalk and then sprinted up the flight of stairs to the two-bedroom flat. He loved the noise of the city, the heavy scent of exhaust from the morning rush hour that mingled with a hint of curry from the Indian restaurant across the street, and even the unpredictable spring weather. He'd come a long way from the slums of north London where he'd grown up.

He slammed the front door shut, then settled in at his computer with a cup of hot coffee and a slice of leftover pizza. The way things were progressing with Mr. Taylor, he'd soon be able to invite Miss iPod to dinner at the Crowne Plaza to celebrate. He clicked open his e-mail, anxious to read Mr. Taylor's response to his latest request, this one for seven thousand dollars to be wired to Abraham's account to cover the remaining transfer fees the bank had imposed. A final payment, he promised.

He scanned his in-box.

Nothing.

Abraham frowned. Normally George Taylor was prompt in his replies. If he'd decided to pull out…

Abraham gripped the edges of the keyboard and fought to stop a wave of panic. No. He would stay calm and wait—years of training had taught him that. It took months to gain people's trust so that they were willing to mortgage their homes, take cash advances off their credit cards, sell their cars and even steal. He just needed to be patient.

Abraham blew out a long, slow breath. He had to

reassure Mr. Taylor that everything was still on track, and that his help was essential to the success of the deal.

The retired Dallas engineer had already wired him thousands of dollars to cover various bogus transaction fees. Abraham had assured him that paying these fees would release assets worth millions once belonging to a dead government official from West Africa. The deal would go through, Abraham told himself—Mr. Taylor had invested too much to simply back out now.

He began drafting another e-mail. The con was far from over. Mr. Taylor deserved the chance to see the money himself. Soon, it would be waiting in a hotel room in London in a silver suitcase, with hired guards on each side. Abraham's smile returned. Thirty-one million dollars in cash wasn't all that would be waiting for George Taylor.

# ONE

Lindsey Taylor wondered exactly how many faux pas she'd be committing by taking off her three-inch sling backs, sneaking across the terrace and stealing into the library for a short reprieve from her best friend Sarah's wedding reception. At the moment, both feet felt as if she'd just attempted to run a marathon. And after an extended ceremony, dozens of photos and an hour and a half of socializing, it was no wonder.

Still, barring the problematic issues of her attire, Sarah and Brad's wedding had been a success. The decision to hold the ceremony in the enclosed garden behind Sarah's parents' luxurious North Dallas home hadn't gone over well at first. But, with a bit of help from a wedding coordinator, the landscaped area had been transformed into an elegant wedding and reception venue. Even Sarah's mother had agreed that the setting—while far from traditional in her mind—was perfect for a summer ceremony.

Lindsey winced as a stab of pain shot from the ball of her foot to her calf. The sight of the four-tiered chocolate wedding cake on the other side of the terrace clinched the decision. No one would miss the maid of honor for thirty minutes or so. And after enjoying some solitude with a thick slice of cake and the book she was reading, she'd be ready to join society again.

She made her way through the throng of guests toward the house, but crossing the tiled decking around the pool gracefully turned out to be an exercise in futility. Her ankle twisted, and she barely caught herself before sprawling into the pool. She teetered for a moment on the narrow heels, then righted herself, glancing up to see if anyone had caught her near mishap.

Best man Kyle Walker waved at her from the other side of the pool.

Great. She felt her cheeks redden as she forced a smile and waved back. Kyle was just as handsome as he'd been in college. Even more so, in fact. Clean shaven, short dark hair and that one familiar dimple on his left cheek, not to mention the classy tuxedo…

Memories of tutoring sessions, final exams and football games came flooding back. Lindsey and Sarah had met Kyle and Brad as freshmen at University of Texas. The four of them had become fast friends but Lindsey had lost track of Kyle after she left school. Apparently Sarah's recent reconnection with him, followed by her engagement to Brad after a decade apart, had sparked an interest in matchmaking. Sarah had even gone as far as to suggest how romantic it would be if Lindsey and Kyle were to discover love after all these years.

Except she and Kyle had never been anything more than friends. And any matchmaking attempts had fallen between the cracks of last-minute wedding preparations and Kyle's delayed flight into Dallas last night. There simply hadn't been time for the two of them to chat.

But while Lindsey had no intention of romanticizing their long-overdue reunion, perhaps her escape to the library could wait.

Margie Adams, mother of the bride, waylaid Lindsey halfway across the terrace, balancing two plates of cake and a cup of punch in her hands. "You were right, Lindsey."

"I was?" Lindsey squeezed her sequined purse under her arm, taking the cake Mrs. Adams offered.

"I thought a chocolate cake with chocolate frosting would be completely inappropriate for the wedding, but it's absolutely fantastic," Mrs. Adams said, taking a bite. "Don't tell a soul, but I'm on my second piece. You've simply got to try it."

Lindsey took a bite. "This is delicious."

Mrs. Adams wiped the edge of her mouth with a cream-colored napkin embossed with Sarah's and Brad's names. "And another thing, Lindsey. I wanted to tell you that you look absolutely stunning tonight. That old adage of 'always a bridesmaid, never a bride' certainly isn't true. Soon we'll be planning your ceremony."

Lindsey frowned. Suddenly the cake didn't seem quite so appetizing. Why was it that everyone believed that being single was a matter of fate and not choice? She'd been a bridesmaid in three different wedding parties in the past two years and someone had made a similar comment to her at every wedding.

Lindsey pressed her lips together. "You know, Mrs. Adams, while I do plan to marry one day, I'm really not in any hurry—"

Mrs. Adam's held up her free hand. "I know, my dear, I know. Even Sarah waited until her thirties to marry. But one can't wait forever, especially if you want a family…."

Lindsey took another bite of cake, while Mrs. Adams continued her monologue on the importance of finding the right mate. Sarah's mom tended to ramble—and eat—when she was nervous, and apparently the wedding of her only daughter had catapulted her into that precarious frame of mind.

Lindsey glanced across the terrace for a glimpse of Kyle, but he'd disappeared. Not that it mattered, of course. She took another bite of cake, trying to ignore the pain in her feet, and turned back to Mrs. Adams. Apparently it was going to be a very long night.

Kyle leaned down to kiss Sarah on the cheek. "Congratulations, you two. This evening turned out perfectly."

Brad thumped him on the upper arm. "Now it's your turn, buddy."

"For marriage?" Kyle coughed. "One of these days, but I've got too much on my plate right now."

Unfortunately, a relationship took time, which was something he had far too little of right now. Between running his own company and opening up a new office in Dallas, finding time for a serious relationship had fallen off his to-do list.

"Trust me, Kyle. When the right woman comes along, you'll find the time." Brad wrapped his arm around his bride's waist. "Besides, do you see me worrying about work? There's more to life, you know. And a few extra perks like marriage can't hurt."

Sarah pulled away from Brad's embrace, her hands on her hips. "So you see me as a perk, Mr. O'Conner?"

"The only perk I'll ever need, Mrs. O'Conner." Brad wrapped his arms around Sarah, who melted into his embrace as they kissed.

Kyle cleared his throat. "I think I'll leave the two of you to your blissful state of matrimony."

"Wait a minute, Kyle," Sarah said, stopping him from escaping. "You've had a chance to talk to Lindsey, haven't you?"

Kyle shook his head. "Nothing more than a quick 'hi, it's good to see you again.' Every time I head her direction, she's deep in conversation with someone."

"That's no excuse."

Kyle laughed. It hadn't been an excuse. Not really, anyway. It was just that thirteen years changed a person, and picking up from the last day he'd seen her wasn't exactly easy.

"I always thought the two of you were perfect for each other," Sarah continued.

"We were friends. Nothing more."

Sarah nodded across the terrace. "At least go rescue her from my mother. You remember how much my mother talks. She'll keep her half the night, and Lindsey's too polite to say anything."

Kyle glanced at Lindsey, smiling to himself as he remembered the first time they met. He'd been pulling a load of pink clothes from a Laundromat washing machine, after accidentally tossing a pair of new red jogging shorts into the mix. Then Lindsey had walked in. A trip to the supermarket and two hours later, she'd somehow managed to turn his socks and T-shirts white again.

A decade or so later, she still looked beautiful even if the pink bridesmaid dress she wore might be a tad frilly for his tastes. Slender frame, honey-colored hair pulled up in a classic twist, big brown eyes... He'd often wondered what would have happened if their friendship had turned into something more all those years ago.

His cell phone vibrated in his jacket, stopping his reminiscing. He glanced at the text message and frowned. "Emergency in Amsterdam. Call D.C."

Great. Matt's timing couldn't be worse, but Kyle knew he couldn't ignore the message. Security breaches were a serious cause for concern, and he was afraid there was either a mole in their Amsterdam office or a bug in their computer software. Both posed a threat to the integrity of the company that couldn't wait.

"Please don't tell me you're working," Sarah said.

Kyle flashed her an apologetic smile. "It will only take a few minutes. You don't mind if I step inside the house and make a call, do you?"

Sarah shrugged in defeat. "Try the library. It should be quiet in there."

He heard Lindsey's soft laugh as he headed inside. He would definitely make an effort to talk to her before the night was out.

By the time Lindsey heard the ominous crack, it was too late.

Her first mistake had been to agree to wear the pink

taffeta bridesmaid's dress with the layers of ruffles down the back. The second mistake had been the shoes—one of the silver heels had just snapped off like a dry twig. Her left hip jutted forward and punch splashed over the edge of her glass, dribbling down the front of her dress. Teetering on one foot, she struggled to keep her balance and avoid spilling the rest of the drink onto the beige suede couch in front of her. The book under her arm slapped against the floor of the small library, followed by her purse. A groan escaped her lips as she grabbed for the couch. Fortunately, she was still holding the generous slice of cake with an inch of chocolate frosting.

"Need some help?"

Lindsey's arm jerked at the sound of a voice inside the darkened room. The cake flipped off the plate, into the air, and landed smack-dab in the middle of Kyle's white tuxedo shirt. It was clearly too late for help. She looked at him, horrified, and wondered if it was physically possible to dissolve into the expensive Oriental rug on the library floor.

"I am so sorry," she said, setting the drink and now-empty plate on the coffee table. "I didn't know anyone was in here."

Lindsey bit her lower lip, wondering how in the world she had managed to make a complete fool out of herself in less than five seconds. Kyle's familiar smile—though lovely to look at—did nothing to erase her humiliation.

A wave of heat flooded her cheeks as he reached for the empty plate and used it to scrape some of the brown frosting from his white shirt.

"I really am sorry," she said again.

"Don't worry about it. This was heading to the cleaners tomorrow anyway. And better my shirt than Mr. Adams's suede couch." He flashed her another wide grin. "Besides, I was hoping we'd get a chance to chat before I have to fly back home to D.C."

"Me, too." She couldn't help but match his smile as she sat down. "It's been a long time."

"Thirteen years to be exact."

He was right, though she could barely believe it. Another decade, an extra pound or two, a handful of gray hairs she ensured were professionally colored every six weeks...

"Did you really have to bring up the fact that it's been that long?"

He settled into the couch across from her. "Would it help if I told you that you look even better thirteen years later?"

"Only if it were true," she countered.

"Oh, it definitely is."

He always had known how to say the right thing, possessing enough charm to rival Prince Charming himself.

"Did I mention how good it is to see you again?" She reached down to examine what remained of her seventy-five-dollar heels and moaned at the ruined shoe. He picked up her book and purse, handing them to her. "Thanks. I didn't know that the best man's job description included taking care of the maid of honor."

"Not a bad description in my opinion. Trying to escape the wedding reception?"

Lindsey squeezed the paperback into her purse. "My feet are killing me, and I didn't think anyone would notice if I slipped out for thirty minutes. Of course, I didn't expect you to beat me to my favorite hideout."

"Your favorite hideout?"

She looked at the wall-to-wall bookshelves filled with everything from Grisham to Hemingway to Peretti. "I'm still a bit of a bookaholic, and Sarah's father has always given me unlimited access to this room."

"Now that you mention it, I don't think I can ever remember seeing you without a book." He stole a glance at his computer. "If we're confessing, I suppose I have to admit to becoming a bit of a workaholic the past few years."

"I'd say so." The blue light of a laptop glowed on the coffee table. Lindsey's brow furrowed. "Working during your best friend's wedding reception?"

"An emergency in Amsterdam." His smile faded. "Looks bad, doesn't it?"

She dismissed his concern with a wave of her hand, ignoring her gut reaction. Just because her father had taken up permanent residency inside the World Wide Web didn't mean Kyle was also stuck there. This situation was completely different. Kyle had to make a living.

Lindsey slid forward to the edge of the couch to unbuckle the strap of her broken shoe, mentally reviewing what Sarah had told her about Kyle.

First of all, he was still single. She could practically hear Sarah's voice in her head, announcing the fact.

Secondly, Kyle lived in D.C., splitting his time between Washington and London with an occasional trip to Hong Kong or Eastern Europe. The fact that he lived halfway across the country removed any pressure.

After tonight, they'd probably never see each other again. Considering she'd just dumped a half pound of chocolate frosting on his shirt, he was probably glad.

Thirdly, Sarah had told her that he was extremely successful, running his own security company. This was a plus to many single girls, but it wasn't high up on her list. Money was nice, but she wasn't going to fall for a bank account even if there was a handsome man attached.

The bottom line was, while she might be tired of always being a bridesmaid, she was even more tired of the constant matchmaking schemes of Sarah and her other friends. Perhaps being single was simply God's plan for her life.

Lindsey held up the broken heel and shook her head. She undid the second sling back and plopped her feet up on the coffee table. "Sarah told me you've gone into the security business."

Kyle started shutting down his laptop. "I spent a few years working in international finance and couldn't believe how lax security was. I saw a hole in the market and decided to start a company. We deal primarily in fraud investigation and financial security systems. We're just now expanding here in Dallas, so this visit is part business, part pleasure."

"Sounds like an interesting line of work," she said, thinking that she wasn't the slightest bit surprised that he'd made something of himself.

"The hours are a bit crazy some days, but I love the travel perks. Sarah told me you're working for an adoption agency?"

She tucked a stray strand of hair behind her ear. "Not

quite as exciting as seeing the world, but I feel as if I make a difference."

"I'm sure you do," he said.

Lindsey looked away from those intense sea-blue eyes and tried to convince herself that the odd feeling in her stomach had everything to do with the romantic atmosphere of her best friend's wedding—and nothing to do with being in the same room with Kyle Walker. Or perhaps the salmon hors d'oeuvres she'd indulged in from the buffet weren't agreeing with her.

She shot him another glance and saw him looking at her intently. She felt her breath catch and that odd feeling swelled. Was it possible that for once Sarah's intuitions had been on target?

Kyle was surprised that an hour and a half had already passed. He and Lindsey had swapped story after story as they caught up on the past few years. He'd forgotten how much he used to enjoy being around her, talking to her. The unique way she interpreted life had always captivated him.

"The last time I saw you, you were making plans to intern in D.C. for the summer. Did you ever go?" she asked.

"Yes, and I ended up working for that same firm after graduation." He lost his train of thought for a second as he admired her toffee-colored eyes. "And the last time I saw you, if I remember correctly, you had just received an A minus on your algebra final."

"All thanks to you and your brilliant tutoring. Fortunately for everyone, my career has little to do with mathematics." With her bare feet propped up on the coffee table, she looked content and relaxed. "College seems like a lifetime ago, doesn't it?"

He nodded. All except for that one day when he'd looked across a pile of math books at her and suddenly wondered what it would be like to kiss her. He'd be risking their friendship, but he thought it might be worth it. But before he'd had a chance to act on the notion, her mother's cancer diagnosis had whisked her out of school. Out of school and out of his life. Missing his chance with Lindsey was one of his few regrets.

And now, all these years later, she was sitting across from him again, making him want to forget the urgent phone call from his coworker, Monday's business meeting downtown and more importantly, the fact that he lived a thousand miles away. He hadn't expected that seeing her again would dredge up these feelings and remind him of the dozens of times he'd wondered what would have happened if he'd asked her out all those years ago.

"The Star-Spangled Banner" played, jolting him back to reality.

Lindsey rummaged through her purse and then held up her cell phone. "You don't mind, do you?"

"Not at all."

He watched while she took the call, making a determined effort to rein in his unruly emotions. Somewhere between listening to his best friend say "I do" and watching him kiss his bride, Kyle had dropped off the edge of insanity. His life was fine. Complete. He didn't need a woman to find happiness. He caught another glimpse of her beautiful eyes and wondered at the truth of that statement.

Lindsey's face was pale as she flipped the phone shut.

Kyle leaned forward, sensing something was wrong. "What's up?"

"That was the hospital. My father's just been taken to the emergency room."

# TWO

Kyle watched as Lindsey grabbed for her purse, her hands shaking as she stumbled to her feet. "I'm sorry. I've got to go."

"Whoa. Slow down." He jumped up from the couch. "You're not going out anywhere by yourself."

"I'll be all right." She slung her purse across her shoulder. The rosy blush she'd had all evening had completely disappeared from her face. "Apparently he fell and hit his head."

"You're in no condition to drive." He slid his laptop into his black leather briefcase before snatching up his tuxedo jacket. "I can drive you to the hospital and then take a taxi back to my hotel once I know everything's okay."

She stared at his shirt, tears suddenly glistening on her eyelashes. "Are you sure?"

He stopped himself from reaching out to touch her cheek. "Trust me. Even if they're still here, which I doubt, Sarah and Brad won't miss either of us."

"You have a point." She cocked her head. "What about your shirt?"

He glanced down at the chocolate smear, then pointed to the shoes she'd just picked up off the floor. "I'd say neither of us will win a prize in the best-dressed category."

Her faint smile brought a tinge of color back to her cheeks. "I'll go grab another pair from Sarah's bedroom."

"Good. I'll let someone know where we're going. I'll meet you back down here in a couple minutes."

The relief that washed over her face made him glad he'd been with her when the call came in. It also made him realize how much he'd missed her. And how much he didn't want their time together to end.

He glanced at his watch. Nine forty-five. The hour time change from D.C. would make the late night even later for him, but he could grab a couple hours of extra sleep in the morning. All that mattered right now was getting Lindsey to her father.

Five minutes later, they were speeding down the freeway toward the hospital. Lindsey sat beside him, her fingers nervously toying with the strap of her purse. "I appreciate you doing this for me. You were right. I don't think I could have driven."

"It's not a problem. It gives me a chance to see a bit of the city."

Lindsey's soft laugh filled the car. It was a laugh he'd like to hear more of. "I can think of prettier cities at night, but you're a sport."

He switched to the fast lane, thankful traffic was light for a Friday night. "Tell me what happened with your mother."

Her heavy sigh caused him to wonder if he'd brought up the wrong topic. Upsetting her further was the last thing he wanted to do. "I'm sorry. It's none of my business—"

"No, no, it's fine. My mother's cancer went into remission for several years, and then came back pretty aggressively. She died four years ago."

"I'm so sorry, Lindsey."

"I still miss her a lot, but I've come to accept that she's in a better place."

"And your father? I always liked him. How is he?"

Her gaze drifted out the window. "For the most part, he was coping pretty well, until about eight or nine months ago."

"What happened then?"

"He was diagnosed with prostate cancer. His prognosis is good, but I'm worried about him." The lights of a passing semi caught her grave expression. "He's become detached. And he's concerned about money even though he has a sizable retirement fund."

"Does he go out much?"

She shook her head. "Not anymore. He used to be involved with church and the local Rotary Club, but I think his friends have pretty much given up on him."

Kyle let up on the accelerator and changed lanes again to allow a speeding car to pass him. "How does he spend his time?"

"On the Internet. And watching television." She motioned for him to take the next exit. "I invite him to go places with me as often as I can, but most of the time he comes up with an excuse to not go. He wouldn't even come to Sarah's wedding."

Kyle flipped on his turn signal and eased onto the exit ramp. The red glow of the emergency entrance announced the hospital ahead. His grip tightened on the steering wheel as memories of his last visit to the E.R. flashed before him.

"What about your family?" she asked.

"My parents retired to Florida and love it. My sister actually lives here in Dallas with her husband and twin daughters. I'm planning to have dinner with them tomorrow night. I don't see them near as often as I'd like."

"Sarah told me that your brother, Michael…" Her voice trailed off, as if she didn't know how to finish the sentence.

Kyle swallowed. "He died about six years ago."

"I'm sorry, Kyle," she said, her voice full with sympathy.

"It was a shock to all of us." He pulled up at the emergency entrance, glad to have a reason to change the subject. "I'll park the car and meet you at the patient-information desk, okay?"

"Okay. Thanks."

He met her ten minutes later and told her where he'd parked. "Any word on your father's condition?"

She slipped the ticket into her purse. "I saw him briefly. They've admitted him for observation, which is standard for a head injury. Plus, his blood pressure's elevated as well as his heart rate. But hopefully he'll be able to go home tomorrow."

Kyle shoved his hands into his front pockets. "Do you want me to stay with you for a while?"

She shook her head. "You've done so much already, Kyle, and you've got to be exhausted. I'll be fine. Really."

He wondered if she regretted not being able to prolong the evening as much as he did. "I enjoyed tonight. Even the chocolate frosting."

"Me, too. It's been too long." She pushed the elevator button.

"Yeah, it has. I guess this is goodbye, then. It was great to see you again, Lindsey."

"You, too, Kyle."

"If ever you're in the D.C. area, look me up."

"I will."

Neither of them said anything for a moment. He considered asking her out for dinner, but something stopped him. She had her own life to live in Dallas, while he had his in D.C. Another evening spent together wouldn't change that. It was time to put the past behind him.

The elevator dinged and a group of nurses stepped out. Clearing his throat, he dug into his wallet, pulled out a business card and handed it to her before the elevator door closed. "I'll be in the area a few more days on business. If you need something…anything…just call me."

Lindsey took in a deep, calming breath and tried not to lose her temper. What she needed was a way to knock some sense into her father. From the moment she'd arrived in his hospital room, all he'd done was insist she go check on his cat. It wasn't that she didn't want to help—not at all. But it was late and the last thing she was worried about was Sammy, his Siamese feline. She glanced down at her father's groggy visage and swallowed her frustration. She might as well indulge him. It was the least she could do.

She leaned over and pushed back a strand of curly gray hair from his forehead. He'd aged the past few months, and it had her worried. Something had to be done.

He squeezed her hand. "So you'll go?"

She smiled and nodded. "Yes, Daddy, I'll go. Can't have you worrying about Sammy, now, can we?"

He knew she'd do anything for him. He was all the family she had, and despite the fact that he drove her crazy, she loved him fiercely.

Fifteen minutes later, Lindsey parked alongside the curb of her father's ranch-style, brick home and shut off the engine. The neighborhood was relatively safe, but she still didn't like being here alone at night. She stepped out of the car, locked the doors and set the alarm.

It was quiet. Too quiet.

*I know you're here, Lord. I just need an extra measure of your peace tonight.*

She crossed to the mailbox and slipped in the key she carried in her purse. These days, her father didn't even bother bringing in the mail and the box was always full. Pulling out a stack of envelopes, she tried to get a grip on her emotions. Her tattered nerves were ridiculous. It had simply been an emotional, draining day, between Sarah's wedding and her father's emergency trip to the hospital.

And Kyle.

She managed a smile. No. Seeing Kyle again after all these years had been the highlight of her day. Maybe even of her week.

A shadow lengthened against the walkway as she turned toward the house. She froze at the curb. Something rustled in the bushes that lined the front of her dad's house.

Suddenly, a cat darted out of the bushes. She jumped back, smacking her arm against the side of the mailbox. The cat ran across the yard and out of sight.

Her heart pounded. She clutched the mail to her chest and hurried to the house. Cat or no cat, she'd had enough surprises for one day.

Lindsey opened the front door, turned off the alarm, then locked the door behind her as she called for Sammy. It bothered her that her father seemed more worried about Sammy than the fact that he had just been admitted into the hospital. Or the fact that his only daughter was tromping around late at night to check on an animal that was more than likely sound asleep at the foot of his bed.

Taking a deep breath to calm herself, she walked past the ten-gallon fish tank and dropped the pile of mail onto her father's orderly rolltop desk that sat in the corner of the living room. The top envelope caught her eye. She picked up the letter.

Regional Recovery Agency. A collection agency?

Her eyes narrowed. Why in the world was her father receiving mail from a collection agency? She opened the top-right drawer of his desk where she knew he kept his mail. There was a stack of opened notices all from the same company. She shook her head. There had to be a mistake. Her father had a perfect credit record. Or so she'd always assumed. He hated debt and had always worked to ensure she felt the same way.

She went to the open-planned kitchen, separated from the living room by a bar, and poured herself a glass of water. In the morning, all this would make sense. Her father would be released and he'd explain.

Except how could he explain a pile of letters from bill collectors? She set her glass down on the counter with a thud.

*Identity theft?*

The thought knocked the wind out of her. Was it possible? She went back to his desk and sat down. All the time he spent online didn't ensure that he was knowledgeable about keeping passwords and credit-card numbers safe. There were so many predators out there these days that even regular mail wasn't safe anymore.

Lindsey began flipping through the letters one by one. Bill collectors meant that the problem was substantial and couldn't be solved overnight. She could call Kyle tomorrow. He would definitely know a thing or two about identity theft.

She rubbed the back of her neck and glanced around the room. Everything looked exactly the way it had when she'd dropped by three days ago with a dish of homemade lasagna and a loaf of garlic bread. The *TV Guide* and crossword puzzle lay on the armrest of her father's recliner; the stack of CDs were neatly piled beside his stereo. Coffee-table books, her mother's afghan and his worn slippers all lay in their rightful places. Even the fish tank, with its colorful African cichlids, still looked crystal clear.

Everything would be fine tomorrow, she told herself. They'd work through this just as they had worked through his diagnosis with prostate cancer. The doctors had given him an eighty-five-percent chance of a complete recovery. Surely the odds of solving this were even higher. She started toward the hallway to search for Sammy and then stopped short on the beige shag carpet. She stared at the glass curio cabinet against the wall, which had been a gift from her father to her mother on their thirtieth wedding anniversary.

The curio cabinet was empty. Every single one of her mother's expensive porcelain figurines was gone. All of them. Lindsey opened the cabinet door and ran her finger across the dusty shelf. It couldn't be. Her father would never sell the collection her mother had worked on for over four decades.

Would he?

# THREE

Sammy strutted up to Lindsey and rubbed against her legs. She picked up the cat and held him against her chest, staring at the empty cabinet. Nothing made sense. Not the missing curios. Not the pile of collection notices. Nothing.

She put Sammy down despite his protests and shut the cabinet door. She crossed the room to her father's desk. Two wooden file cabinets stood beside it, a glossy-leafed spider plant perched on the closest one. The other was covered with a half-dozen photos, mostly of her—one of the hazards of being an only child. Her first birthday…Disneyland when she was eleven… high-school graduation…standing in front of the Eiffel Tower while on vacation in France…the last family picture taken before her mother died…

She bit her lip and stared at her mother's familiar smile. Her father had always claimed she and her mother could have been sisters with their curly blond hair and matching wide smiles. She stared at the photo. What would her mother do if she were here right now? Rush to the hospital to demand an explanation from her father? Or sort though his desk for answers?

Lindsey pressed her hands against the back of the rolling desk chair, wishing her mother were here. She sat down and pulled open the middle desk drawer. Half a dozen black pens lay side by side next to a neat pile of paper clips, rubber bands, Post-it Notes and a stapler. The left-hand drawer had hanging files. Hesitating slightly, she flicked the tab of the first file. More than likely, her father would have a few choice words for her if he knew she was perusing his desk, but she felt she had no choice. The answer had to be here.

She scanned each file folder. Appliance manuals. Car-service records. Investment figures. Receipts, warranties and phone bills. She tugged the drawer open farther to get to the back. Tax papers. Travel brochures. And…bingo. A fat folder all the way in the back revealed a three-inch-thick, rubber-banded batch of letters from collection agencies.

Nausea washed over her as she dumped the file onto the floor, slid off the sandals she had borrowed from Sarah and slumped down onto the carpet cross-legged beside them. She pulled out one of the folded pieces of correspondence to scan the contents of the letter. "You currently have an outstanding balance"…"Our policy requires all balances be paid in full"…"Please remit payment within ten days of receiving this letter…"

The next dozen envelopes revealed more of the same. Follow-up letters, threats and carefully chosen words of intimidation. Halfway through the pile the news got even worse, if that were possible. "We have initiated legal action and are preparing a lawsuit…"

A lawsuit?

The air rushed out of Lindsey's lungs, and she fought

to catch her breath. It was one thing to deal with the ramifications of possible identity theft, but a lawsuit? How could her father have let it come to this? For thirty-five years, he'd worked as a project engineer with a large oil company and brought home a good living. His investments had grown steadily throughout the years, giving him enough for a comfortable retirement. Now his retirement was in danger. Why hadn't he told her about this?

Lindsey worked to fight the growing queasiness. Whatever was happening to her father had gone beyond a few late payments to a credit-card company. Had he gone to the police or hired a lawyer? The process might be slow, but surely he had enough evidence to verify his innocence while the issue was being resolved.

Unless this *was* his fault.

No. That was impossible. Lindsey stuffed the last notice back onto the pile and slipped the rubber band around the envelopes. There was no dismissing the fact that her father was in serious financial trouble, but it couldn't have been his fault. She reached into her pocket and fingered the business card Kyle had given her. He'd said to call if she needed something.

The wooden clock sitting above the fireplace mantel chimed midnight, serving as a reminder that it was too late to ask for a favor. Besides, he'd already done enough for her by leaving the wedding reception early to drive her to the hospital. Maybe tomorrow, when things didn't look so bad, she'd call him and ask for his advice.

Sammy was standing in front of his bowl at the far side of the kitchen, demanding his supper, when her cell phone rang. She jumped up and grabbed it out of her bag, terrified that it was the hospital calling to tell her that her father...

"Hello?"

"Lindsey? This is Kyle."

"Kyle?" Her heart skipped a beat. "Hey. You should be sound asleep by now."

"I know I shouldn't have called so late, but I was worried. I didn't wake you, did I?" he asked.

"No. It's fine. I'm glad you called." Sammy brushed up against her legs impatiently. "I'm at my father's house."

She pressed the phone against her shoulder as she crossed the kitchen and bent down to pick up Sammy's bowl.

"Is your father all right?"

"I think he'll be fine." She put the bowl on the counter, opened a can of cat food and spooned the pâté-like substance into the silver bowl. "They're still running some tests, but we should know more tomorrow. At least he's stabilized."

"I'm glad to hear that."

"Me, too. The only thing is..." She hesitated as she put Sammy's bowl on the floor. "You deal with identity theft in your company, don't you?"

"Sure. I'd say a good ten to fifteen percent of our clients are dealing with compromised finances." There was a pause on the line. "Why do you ask?"

"I think someone stole my father's identity. It's the only explanation I can come up with for what I've found," she said, feeling a wave of guilt for sharing her father's secrets.

In any other circumstances, she'd be thrilled to talk

to Kyle, but at the moment, she had the strong urge to hang up. Saying it out loud made it all too real.

"Tell me exactly what you found," he said calmly.

Lindsey drew in a steadying breath. "My father was worried about his cat, so I promised I'd drop by the house. On my way in, I checked the mail and found letters from a collection agency."

"Anything else?"

"I found more notices in his desk. At least two dozen letters from several agencies." She picked up the dishrag and began wiping the already spotless countertop. "And there's more."

"Tell me," he said.

"My mother has a collection of limited-edition porcelain figurines worth quite a bit of money. She's been collecting them for years." She glanced at the empty cabinet across the room. "They're all missing."

"Could your father have sold them to pay down his debt?"

"It's possible, but it doesn't fit." She dropped the rag into the sink, then slid onto one of the bar stools at the end of the counter. "My father's a miser when it comes to money. He's never late on credit-card payments. In fact, he refuses to use credit in most cases. I can't even see him having debt, never mind selling the curios to pay it off."

"You mentioned how he'd been depressed lately. Could it be he's overspending online, or maybe gambling?"

"Gambling? I don't know." She squeezed her eyes shut. This couldn't be happening.

"Lindsey, I know it's a sensitive topic, but it does happen. Spending money online becomes addictive. And it's a way to bury the pain of loss."

Lindsey couldn't even respond. Was her father spending his retirement money online to cope with his grief? How could she have missed this?

"I'm sorry," Kyle said. "I know it's none of my business."

"No, it's okay." She rubbed her thumb against her temples and took another breath. "I'm scared, Kyle. There was even mention of a lawsuit in one of the letters."

"I know it's frightening. Especially if it is identity fraud. I can't do much tonight, but with a few more details and your father's permission—"

"I'm not sure he'll give you that," she said, looking at the stack of letters on the floor.

"You have to know that admitting what's happening is often the most difficult step," Kyle continued. "It makes a person feel out of control. Vulnerable. And the solution isn't always easy. Trying to clear his name will be time-consuming and tedious. He'll need you more than ever to deal with the cleanup."

"What if it *is* his fault? What if you're right and he's taken up online gambling and bought a yacht off eBay or…or a time-share in Tahiti?"

His laugh made her smile. "Let's find out what the damage is first. Then we'll worry about the solution."

She knew she shouldn't be dragging him into this situation, but she didn't know who else to turn to. She picked up her car keys off the counter and fiddled with the key chain. "I'm sorry to dump all this on you, Kyle. I'm sure you didn't have this conversation in mind when you called."

"I was thinking of something more along the lines of asking you to dinner, actually."

Her smile widened. "Dinner would be nice, Kyle. I—"

Lindsey was interrupted by the violent sound of shattering glass.

She jumped from the bar stool and spun around. The metal handle on the back door shook. Someone was breaking in.

# FOUR

Kyle drove as fast as he could without risking getting pulled over. Lindsey's directions had been surprisingly simple, a blessing considering he knew his way around Dallas about as well as he knew his way around the kitchen. With any luck, he should be there in the next five minutes.

*Except five minutes might be too late.*

He pushed the redial button on his cell phone but she still wasn't picking up. He'd told her to get out of the house through the front door and wake up one of the neighbors while he called 911. He glanced again at the clock on the dashboard. The police should be there by now.

*God, please don't let anything happen to her.*

He couldn't help but wonder if the break-in had something to do with the pile of collection notices she'd told him about. What exactly had George Taylor gotten himself involved in? The bottom line was that the circumstances were no longer a threat only to him. There was a good chance his actions had put his daughter's life on the line. Kyle knew Lindsey wasn't someone who would back down from a situation just because things got rough. But he had a feeling things were going to get even rougher.

His tires squealed as he took the next exit too sharply, and skidded to a stop at the light. He pounded the steering wheel out of frustration, wondering if he should ignore the red light. Another car idled beside him, but other than that the road was quiet. The digital clock announced another minute had passed. The light turned green. He slammed his foot against the accelerator and shot through the intersection. Now all he needed to do was to find the third street on the left.

The area quickly transformed from strip malls and late-night diners to residences. Stately oak trees, merely shadows in the pale moonlight, lined either side of the winding road. He passed the first left. It couldn't be far now.

The piercing shrill of a siren tore into the quiet of the late night. Kyle glanced in his rearview mirror, jerked his foot off the accelerator and pulled to the side of the road. Strobing red lights pressed in behind him.

*No, God. No…*

His chest constricted. The ambulance shot by, casting eerie flickers of light across his dash. He moved back into the lane and picked up speed, waiting to see if it was headed for Lindsey's father's house. He tried to block the flood of images that flipped through his mind. What were the chances of her fending off an attacker before the police arrived?

The emergency vehicle whizzed down the road, passing Mr. Taylor's street. Kyle felt the rush of adrenaline shoot through his heart. *It wasn't her. It wasn't her.*

Slowing down at the third turn, he swung a sharp

left and began searching for the house. Thirty-three... thirty-five... He stopped two houses short of her father's one-story brick house and pulled his rented Mazda against the curb.

*Please, God. Let her be okay.*

He steadied his breathing. Half a dozen people stood talking on the front lawn, but the street lamp didn't cast enough light to clearly make out who they were. One or two officers and a couple of neighbors? Squinting in the darkness through the windshield, he caught a glimpse of Lindsey's pink dress and let out a sigh of relief.

*Thank you, Lord.*

He got out of the car and approached the scene slowly. The last thing he needed was to be marked as a possible suspect.

One of the officers stepped toward him and held out an arm. "I'm going to have to ask you to stop right there, sir."

Kyle froze in his tracks, holding his hands away from his sides. "I'm a friend of Lindsey—"

"It's all right, Officer." Lindsey came up beside the uniformed man. "This is Kyle Walker. I was talking to him on my cell when the attempted break-in occurred."

The officer nodded and moved aside.

Kyle pulled her into his arms, overwhelmed with relief. Once again, his reaction to her caught him off guard, just as it had when he'd first seen her at the wedding.

He'd felt more like a college sophomore than a thirty-three-year-old. She'd been the reason he hadn't been able to fall asleep at the hotel, and he'd decided to take a chance and call her despite the late hour. Lucky thing he did.

The problem was, he hadn't planned on this distraction. Not this weekend. He needed to focus on his upcoming meeting with one of his biggest clients.

But no matter how busy things were, Lindsey's situation wasn't something he could dismiss. And neither was Lindsey.

Taking a step back, he shoved his hands in the front pockets of his jeans. "You okay?"

"Yeah. The guy scared me to death, but he never made it inside the house."

"You didn't try to play superhero, did you?" Kyle asked, looking her straight in the eye.

"Are you kidding?" She cocked her head and met his gaze. "I was heading for the front door before I hung up the phone with you. Unfortunately, I didn't make a very graceful exit," she said, a tinge of mischief in her voice.

"What do you mean?" His interest was piqued.

"I smashed into my father's ten-gallon fish tank on my way out of the kitchen and knocked it over. Made enough noise to wake the dead."

"Did you hurt yourself?"

"No, but apparently the crash scared away the would-be thief."

"And the fish?"

She hesitated briefly. "Dumped them in the toilet."

He shook his head in disbelief. "Wait a minute. You did what?"

She shrugged, giving him one of her wide smiles. "What can I say? They're freshwater African cichlids from Malawi. My father loves them."

Kyle didn't try to stifle his laugh. "But you stuck them in the toilet?"

"I know. It was a crazy, stupid reflex. They probably won't make it, but what else was I supposed to do?"

Two policemen stepped out of the house and took the steps leading down to the front yard. The tallest officer approached Lindsey, his fists planted solidly on his hips. "We're finished inside, Miss Taylor. Were you planning to spend the night here?"

"No, sir. Like I said, I'd just dropped by to feed my father's cat. Do you think it's safe to leave the house empty?"

"I'd board up the back window. That seems to be the only vulnerable place."

"I'll help you," Kyle offered. "Is there an alarm system in place?"

Lindsey nodded. "Yes, I had it turned off while I was inside."

"More than likely the guy isn't coming back tonight," the officer continued, "but you still need to alert the security company that the door was damaged. And make sure you turn the alarm back on when you leave."

She stood beside Kyle as the four officers made their way to their squad cars and the lingering neighbors trekked across the lawn toward their houses.

A balding man with bifocals and slippers stopped on the sidewalk and then turned to address Lindsey. "I'll be back with the tank water in a couple minutes, Miss Taylor."

Lindsey waved her thanks. "I appreciate it, Mr. Vasquez."

"Tank water?" Kyle folded his arms across his chest.

"I can't exactly leave the fish floating in the toilet all night." She grinned and her eyes sparkled in the yellow light of the street lamp. "He's getting a plastic bag filled with water from his tank so he can bring the fish back to his house."

"That's a good idea," he admitted.

"Why don't you come inside. I'll let you help me board up the window as long as you promise not to laugh at the ten gallons of water I dumped on my father's floor."

His brow furrowed. "What kind of deal is that?"

"One completely to my advantage."

Kyle resisted the urge to push back a curl that had fallen from her pinned-up hair and now brushed against her cheek. If only she didn't look so appealing in her silly ruffled dress and bare feet. But instead of giving in to his impulse, he followed her up the front stairs.

His shoes squished as he stepped onto the soggy carpet. "I never would have imagined ten gallons of water could make such a mess."

"Tell me about it." She shook her head and maneuvered around the shattered fish tank into the living room. "I'll have to send for someone to dry out the carpet tomorrow."

Except for the fish tank and a pile of glass beneath the broken windowpane in the back door, the house was spotless.

Kyle took in the details of the room. While everything was neatly kept, nothing looked new. Half a dozen framed photos on a file cabinet, a few healthy plants and a worn leather lounge chair and matching couch from another era, flanked by heavy wooden side tables. Even the television looked at least twenty years old.

He cleared his throat. "What did the police do while they were here?"

"Besides ask a lot of questions?" Lindsey pointed to the door. "I showed them where the guy tried to get in, and they dusted for prints. But I'm guessing the prints are my father's or mine—the burglar probably used gloves. And he never set foot inside the house, so they don't have much to go on."

He studied the solid-wood door with its nine, etched-glass windowpanes on the top half. The pane closest to the door handle was shattered. The fact that the door had been locked with a key had probably been a deterrent. If Lindsey hadn't been here to scare him off, though, he would have found a way in eventually. But why? What had he wanted?

"Kyle?"

He turned to look at her. "What is it?"

She had a hammer in one hand and a half-dozen nails in the other, and she was staring at his feet. "I thought the chocolate-covered tux shirt was a unique fashion statement, but this…"

He followed her gaze. One brown shoe and one black shoe stared back at him.

"It's my fault once again, I suppose." She let out a chuckle and handed him the hammer. "Have I thanked you for rushing to my rescue once again?"

He quirked his left brow. Was she flirting? If she was, he liked it. "I don't think so."

"Then I should." She glanced up at him beneath long, dark lashes. "Thank you. You don't know how much this means to me."

Nothing like a beautiful woman to turn his world upside down in the course of an evening. "You know you're welcome."

"I'll be right back. I think there's a piece of plywood in the laundry room that we can use."

He watched her disappear around the corner. Washington, D.C., suddenly seemed a lifetime away.

He glanced around the living room again and his grip on the hammer tightened. Something wasn't right here. If George Taylor had been buying enough stuff to not only lose his entire life savings but unleash a pack of bill collectors, there was no evidence of the man's material indulgences. Everything in the house Kyle had seen so far was cared for but far from new. There were no fancy stereo systems, laptops or flat-screen TVs in sight. If anything, Mr. Taylor's surroundings corroborated Lindsey's descriptions of a thrifty and frugal man.

And there were holes in Lindsey's identity-theft theory. Mr. Taylor was an educated man. If he believed someone had stolen his identity, why wouldn't he have gone immediately to the authorities? It didn't make sense. Add to that the missing porcelain pieces and tonight's break-in—

"Kyle?" Lindsey's fingertips brushed against his sleeve.

She held out the board to him, smiling.

"Sorry." He hadn't heard her come back into the room. He looked down at her, wishing they were standing here under different circumstances. This wasn't the way he wanted to get to know her again. "I was just trying to see if I could make sense of any of this. The collection notices, the missing curios and now the attempted burglary…"

Her smile disappeared. "Any theories?"

"At this point only conjectures. I'll need your father's permission to look through his financial statements and computer files."

"Kyle."

He swapped her the hammer and nails for the board and then set it against the door frame to cover the hole. "And I'm following you home when we're done here."

"I know I asked for your help, but you don't have to do any of this. Just because we were friends years ago—"

"I might not have to, but I want to." He pounded in the first nail. His gut told him this was something that went beyond an ugly case of identity theft. A vision of his brother lying in a casket flashed before him. There was no way he was going to let her handle this alone. "I want you to call me tomorrow once you talk to your father. With his help we can get to the bottom of this."

"Do you really think so?"

"Yes, I do." He turned to her and this time couldn't resist the urge to brush back the loose curl that rested on her cheek. "You know, you've hardly changed at all. I remember a beautiful young woman who cared so much for her parents that she left school to help them during a difficult time. Today, I see a woman who'd do anything for her best friend, including wear a pink ruffled dress she probably hates, with three-inch, back-breaking heels. And—" a blush spread across her face as he talked "—who'd risk her own life to save her father's beloved African cyclops."

Lindsey brought her hand to her mouth and laughed. "They're African cichlids, and you've now completely embarrassed me."

"Cichlids. Okay." He matched her grin. "But that doesn't change the fact that you're quite a woman, Lindsey Taylor. You always have been."

# FIVE

Lindsey shifted in the metal hospital chair, wishing she could find a more comfortable position. She stared over the stark white bedsheets at her father's determined gaze and tried to stay calm. She'd always hated hospitals, but today the pale green walls of the room seemed to close in on her. She shut her eyes for a moment, wishing she could block out the constant beeping of the heart monitor and the endless influx of nurses that reminded her of her mother's last days. Except now it was her father in the hospital.

She wondered if the nurses could give him something for his obstinacy.

"Please, Dad. I know this isn't easy for you, but you've got to tell me what's going on. I just want to help."

Her father jabbed with his fork at a piece of pear on his breakfast tray and shook his head calmly. "I've already told you that there's nothing to tell."

Her stomach clenched, and she held back the angry words on the tip of her tongue.

"Dad—"

"Lindsey, please." He held his plastic fork up as if to

emphasize what he was about to say. "I told you there's nothing to worry about."

Nothing to worry about? Right. She gripped the arms of the chair. After Kyle ensured she'd gotten home safely last night, she'd made a cup of tea and tried to get back into the book she was reading, but even the absorbing storyline couldn't pull her away from reality. Next, she'd turned to the Bible—where she probably should have gone first—but even that had done little to ease her concern. She was worried. There was no getting around it.

She took a sip of orange juice from a plastic cup, in no mood to accept his insistent rebuttals. If he wouldn't agree to help her get to the bottom of the situation, she'd call Kyle and search through every last piece of paper in her father's house until she found out the truth.

"Dad…" She sighed heavily, determined to try one last time. "You can't tell me that a stack of letters from collection agencies, and the fact that all of Mom's porcelain pieces are missing, is nothing. So what is it? Has someone stolen your identity? Or maybe…I don't know…have you been gambling online?"

"Gambling?" He stabbed at another piece of fruit, clearly fed up with her questions. "What are you talking about, Lindsey?"

"What am I talking about?" She rubbed her temples with her fingertips. They were going in circles. "I'm talking about the fact that there are attorneys bringing lawsuits against you for starters."

"You shouldn't have gone through my desk." The lines on her father's forehead deepened. "It's none of your business, and I'm finished discussing it."

"You'd have done the same if the situation was reversed and you know it. All I want to do is help."

"How's Sammy?"

She opened her mouth to respond and then shut it in frustration. How was Sammy? So that was it. Subject closed. All evidence denied. He was more worried about his precious cat than his imploding financial situation. Why wouldn't he let her help him?

"Sammy's fine." She took another sip of her juice. She'd go along with the change of subject. For now. "When are they planning to let you go home?"

"Sometime this afternoon." He smoothed out the edges of his white mustache with his fingers. "Why don't you go home and sleep. You look exhausted."

"That's because I was up half the night worried about you."

"I know, pumpkin, and I really do appreciate it." He reached out and grasped her hand, smiling for the first time all morning. "I need you to trust me on this. Sometimes things aren't what they seem, but everything's going to be all right. I promise."

She squeezed her father's hand, wanting to believe him, wanting to believe this was nothing more than a big misunderstanding that would simply disappear. Her gut told her that wasn't true, but arguing with her stubborn father was only making things worse.

He nudged her arm. "Go home, Lindsey. Get some sleep. I'll call you when they release me."

She was tired, but there was no time for a nap. The carpet cleaners would be at his house in an hour, and she still had to do something about the fish tank and the glass pane in the back door. Not wanting to upset him further, she'd decided to hold off telling him about the break-in. Plus, if he thought her life was in danger for any reason, he'd make her promise not to go back to the house. And that was a promise she wasn't willing to make.

She tossed the empty juice cup into the trash can. "Are you sure you'll be all right?"

He nodded. "Positive."

She leaned over the bed to kiss him on the forehead. "I worry about you. I can't help it."

"I'll be fine." He cupped her face between his hands. "You look so much like your mother. She'd be so proud of you. You know that, don't you?"

Lindsey nodded. She missed her mom so much. And if she were here, she'd know what do to.

"I love you, pumpkin."

She blinked back a tear. "I love you, too, Daddy."

Two minutes later she was downstairs in the lobby, punching Kyle's number into her phone.

He answered on the third ring. "Hello?"

"Kyle, it's me. Lindsey," she said, crossing the lobby.

"I wasn't sure you were going to call."

"I didn't have a choice." She stopped just before the automated doors that led outside, hoping her last statement didn't make it sound as if she didn't want to see him. Because she did. Very much.

"I'm sorry. I didn't mean it that way. It's just that my father refuses to discuss the issue and denies there is anything wrong."

He let out a low whistle. "I'm assuming that means he didn't give you permission to search his house?"

"He didn't, but that doesn't matter." Lindsey bit her

lip, already feeling guilty about what she'd decided to do. "I have unlimited power of attorney. He signed all the papers after he was diagnosed with prostate cancer, in case something happened." A young girl stepped through the doors, bringing with her a blast of Texas summer. Lindsey took a step back into the lobby. "You have to know that I'd never take advantage of his trust. But I think it's appropriate for me to use my power of attorney in these circumstances."

"I think you're right."

She squeezed her eyes shut for a moment. One day her father would thank her. They just had to figure out what was going on first.

"Can you meet me back at my father's house?" she asked. "I'll pick up lunch to sweeten the deal."

"I'll be there in half an hour. Is that soon enough?"

"Yeah." She hadn't expected the wave of relief that followed. At least she wasn't in this alone. "I owe you big-time for this."

*Thank you, Lord, for Kyle Walker.*

She hung up and walked over to the ATM on the other side of the automatic doors to withdraw money for lunch. Rummaging through her purse, she remembered she'd left all her usual cards in her dresser drawer yesterday so she wouldn't have to worry about them at the wedding. She sighed, and pulled a debit card for her emergencies-only account from a zippered pocket.

Sliding the card into the slot, she wondered what she and Kyle might find. She noticed her hand was shaking and rested it against the side of the machine, waiting for the bank to process her request. The ATM spit the card back at her.

Card denied. Insufficient funds.

Insufficient funds? Lindsey smacked the machine with the palm of her hand and shoved in the card again. She didn't have time for this.

Thirty seconds later…denied again.

She glanced around the lobby. A dozen people milled about the room and not one of them seemed to notice that she suddenly couldn't breathe. Or that the room was beginning to spin.

This simply couldn't be happening. There should be at least two thousand dollars in her account.

Or rather, *their* account. She shared it with her father.

Kyle jumped off Mr. Taylor's front porch as Lindsey parked the car. The moment she stepped out, he knew she'd been crying.

He hurried toward her. "What happened? Your father, is he—"

"He's fine. As far as the hospital is concerned, anyway."

"What's wrong then?" he asked.

"I don't know what's going on."

She dug into her purse and yanked out the keys to the front door, forcing him to keep up with her as she marched up the walk. Her chin jutted forward, lips pressed into a thin line. It seemed that frustration had morphed into pure anger.

"Lindsey? What's going on?"

"My father and I have a joint savings account. He set it up a couple years ago. Emergency money, he called it. If either of us got in a bind, we could borrow from it." She stomped up the porch stairs and stopped briefly to face him. "I've used it from time to time, always repaying it quickly. I don't think my father's ever used it, because the balance has never dropped below two thousand dollars."

She shoved the house key into the lock, opened the door and deactivated the alarm. "I needed cash for lunch, so I tried to use the card. It was denied because of 'insufficient funds.' And he claims there's nothing wrong."

Her purse smacked against the wall as she tromped over the still-wet carpet. She slung it down on the floor, away from the mess. A Siamese cat rubbed up against her leg, but she ignored its obvious ploy for attention. "I don't think I've ever been so angry in my entire life."

"Hey," Kyle said, setting his hands on her shoulders. "You've got to calm down. We'll find a way to work this all out."

"I need to check the account." She pulled away from him. "I've got to know what happened."

He watched as she turned on her father's computer and waited for the banking page to load, wishing he could do something—anything—to make things okay.

A couple minutes later, she put her head in her hands. "It's true. There's nothing there." She grabbed the cordless phone and started pacing the room. "I'm calling the bank."

"What can I do?"

She glanced up at him. "Should we start with his e-mails? He spends a lot of time online. Maybe there's something there."

Kyle nodded. "And where are his banking records?"

She pointed to the file drawers. "You shouldn't have any trouble. He's a stickler when it comes to organizing his files."

"Consider that a blessing in the midst of all of this." He slid onto the seat she'd vacated in front of the computer. "We might be able to find something quickly."

While she called the bank, he clicked on Mr. Taylor's e-mail. No password. This was going to be even easier than he thought. He tried to focus on the task in front of him instead of worrying about the woman pacing beside him. She was strong, she'd get through this.

The in-box was empty except for some spam about DVDs and summer airline sales. He searched the mail folders, scanning for anything suspicious. Video close-out sales, travel deals, business news…the man didn't even erase his junk mail. He found a few legitimate-looking messages from friends, but perusing those could be a last resort.

The next e-mail was from an Abraham Omah. Kyle stopped. The solicitation e-mail that followed was all too familiar.

A knot began to form in the pit of his stomach. He stared at the screen, forcing himself to concentrate. In the search box, he typed out "Abraham Omah." Ten seconds later, the computer gave him a list of seventy-six separate e-mail transactions.

He'd found what he was looking for.

"The account is empty, Kyle."

He snapped his head up. "Who made the last with-drawal?"

Lindsey set the phone back in its holder. "The manager's going to call me back with the details. Apparently it was an online purchase."

Looking back at the screen, he scrolled down to the first e-mail, from last fall. He hoped his theory wasn't true but the pieces were all beginning to fit. "Who's Abraham Omah?"

She shook her head. "I don't know. Why?"

"There are dozens of messages here from him." He turned around to face her. "This isn't identity theft, Lindsey."

"Then what is it?"

"I want you to read something. It's the first e-mail from Omah, dated eight months ago." He printed the document and handed it to her. "It's a scam letter," he said. "And I believe your father fell for it."

Color drained from her face as she read the letter out loud.

"It is my pleasure writing you. I am Abraham Omah, and I am soliciting for your humble and confidential assistance to take custody of Thirty-one million Dollars (US $31,000,000.00). These funds have been deposited into a confidential security firm in West Africa, and with your help, will be released to you by the said security firm. You will receive twenty percent if you can help us claim this consignment. PLEASE, I need your support for the success of this business venture as well as your utmost confidentiality. PLEASE acknowledge as soon as possible."

Lindsey blinked. "I don't understand."

"That—" he pointed to the letter "—is how the scam starts. The criminal convinces the target that his help is urgently needed to complete a transaction that will make them both extremely rich."

He leaned back in the chair and folded his arms across his chest, wishing there were an easy way to tell her about this. Last year alone these scams cost Americans an estimated two hundred million dollars—and there was no way to measure the emotional cost. George Taylor was only one of thousands of victims.

"Go on," she said, her voice tight.

"It's called an advance fee fraud or a 419 scam. The victim, in this case your father, believes he's been chosen to share a huge fortune in exchange for doing pretty much nothing. When the deal is threatened, he willingly contributes money to ensure the venture succeeds. The only problem is that in the end, there is no money, and he's lost thousands."

Lindsey shook her head, then glanced down at the cat who cried at her feet. "Sammy's not used to being ignored." She dropped the letter onto the bar before stalking into the kitchen. "Just because my father received a letter like that doesn't mean he responded. He'd never fall for such a setup."

"Lindsey, there are dozens of e-mails between your father and Omah."

Lindsey dug for something in the cupboard. "Would you like some coffee?"

It was already almost ninety degrees outside and not much cooler inside—Mr. Taylor probably tried to save a few bucks by keeping the air turned down. But he'd have a cup. For her.

"One sugar, a little milk."

The refrigerator door clicked shut. She slammed the milk down on the counter and caught his gaze. "I want to know exactly how this works."

Kyle smiled. This was the woman he remembered. The one who faced problems head-on.

"Okay, I'll tell you." While she put two mugs of water into the microwave, he opened one of the file-cabinet drawers and began to look for any printed documents relating to the scam. "The intended victim receives an e-mail from an alleged official who represents a foreign government or some agency. In your father's case, the man's name appears to be Abraham Omah, though of course that isn't his real name."

"Then what happens?"

"The fake official offers to transfer millions of dollars into the victim's bank account. Reasons are as varied as the scam, but normally, the idea is to move hidden assets somewhere accessible. Assets, for example, of dead government workers, or maybe from overinvoiced contracts. The scammers promise a twenty-percent take on the deal and request things like bank-account information and telephone numbers, for starters."

The microwave dinged. "And you're telling me that my father fell for this?"

He found what he was looking for near the back—eight months' worth of correspondence with Abraham Omah—including receipts from Western Union showing money transferred overseas—all filed by date. Kyle stood up with one of the signed papers and went to the counter. "Your father would have been sent numerous documents through the mail with official authentic-looking stamps, seals and logos. Over a period of weeks and months, he would have been asked to provide money for various taxes, attorney bills, trans-

action fees or even bribes. These scammers are sharp—
Omah would have waited to ask for money until he
could tell your father trusted him."

"Trusted him? No way." Lindsey dumped a spoonful
of sugar into each mug.

"The evidence suggests otherwise, Lindsey. It's all
here—I've seen it all before." He set the paper on the
counter and reached for the mug she offered him. "It all
boils down to the fact that your father was told that for
a small amount of money up front, he'd receive a
fortune, and he believed it. For some people, it's a
scenario too good to pass up."

Lindsey stared at her coffee. "How much do you
think he lost?"

Kyle pressed his lips together. There was no way of
knowing at this point. He'd had clients who'd lost
anywhere from a couple hundred to over two hundred
thousand. "I don't know."

She grabbed the letter he'd laid on the counter and
started ripping it into pieces.

"What are you doing, Lindsey?" He reached out to
stop her.

She swung away from him and her elbow hit her
coffee mug. It smashed against the kitchen floor.

"Lindsey." Kyle grabbed her wrists, leading her
around the broken shards and out of the kitchen.

"How could he do something like this?" she yelled,
angry tears spilling down her face.

Kyle pulled her into his arms, holding her against his
chest. "I'm so sorry, Lindsey."

Sobs shook her body but she didn't fight to get away.

He held her tightly and waited. When she'd stopped crying, she looked up at him.

"He's lost everything, hasn't he?"

"No, Lindsey," he said, brushing her hair back from her face. "He hasn't lost you."

# SIX

Lindsey fingered the torn pieces of paper and tried to still the pounding of her heart. What had triggered her father's insane acceptance of someone he'd never even met into his personal life? Why would he throw away thousands of dollars, hoping to win a million-dollar jackpot?

She crossed the floor and stopped at her mother's curio cabinet. Outlines of the porcelain figures in the dust on the glass were the only evidence of where they once sat. She squeezed her eyes shut. She could see them all. The dancing ballerina her father had found in a tiny shop in Switzerland. The swan her mother picked out for her fiftieth birthday. The figure of a mother and child.

A wave of fortitude swept through her. Kyle was right. There was no use denying what had happened. The evidence lay scattered in tangible piles across the living-room floor.

Her shallow breathing deepened. She'd fix this. Somehow. She would figure out a way to rescue her father. She went back into the kitchen, grabbed the dustpan and broom and started sweeping. Reaching down to pick up a large shard, she winced as one of the sharp edges grazed her finger. Blood pooled at the tip.

"Hey. Slow down." Kyle snatched a paper towel from the roll and gently grasped her hand, letting the paper absorb the red stain.

She stared up at him as he took care of her hand, gazing at his handsome face. His eyes met hers, and he pulled her into his arms again. She could feel his heart beat against her cheek and for a moment, she felt warm and safe. If only she could stay here for a while and forget all about everything.

But there wasn't time.

She took a step back, burying dizzying emotions that would have to be explored on another day. Right now, she had to find a way to get her father out of this mess.

Kyle cleared his throat and handed her his untouched mug of coffee. The moment between them had vanished. "I want you to sit down and drink this. I'll clean up the mess."

She fumbled with the handle. "I couldn't let you—"

"Yes, you can." He smiled and turned away.

Obeying orders, she pulled out one of the stools and sat down at the bar that separated the kitchen from the dining room, and brought the mug to her lips. She breathed in the rich aroma, and her stomach growled. Loudly.

"You haven't eaten yet today, have you?" He glanced up at her as he swept the shards into the dustpan.

"I had a few sips of OJ at the hospital."

"I'm admittedly a horrible cook—I live on frozen dinners and takeout most time—but I can make a killer omelet if your dad has a few basics in the fridge."

"You're offering to make me breakfast?" Her eyes

widened. "I'm starting to wish I hadn't lost track of you." She felt a blush rush up her cheeks. Did she have to be quite so obvious? She tried to swallow the lump in her throat. "I'm sorry. I—"

"I've always believed that life is too short to beat around the bush." He shot her a grin, then dumped the broken glass into the trash can. "Omelet?"

"Yeah. That would be great." She took a sip of the coffee. "What if last night's break-in had something to do with all of this?"

"I've been thinking about that myself."

He stood in the middle of the kitchen, hands on his hips. "First things first. Frying pan?"

"Bottom right-hand cupboard."

"Oil?"

"Cabinet next to the fridge."

"Salt and pepper?"

Lindsey slid off the bar stool, then stopped at his questioning gaze.

"Where do you think you're going? Sit back down there, young lady, and relax."

She grinned, amazed that he'd managed to make her smile again on a day like this. "Yes, sir."

Kyle proceeded to gather the items he needed. She watched his smooth, fluid movements. He might not be brilliant in the kitchen, but he still looked good in his khaki T-shirt that lay taut against his broad chest.

"Okay. Back to your question." He set the pan on the stove, turned on the burner and started chopping onions. "In the cases I've dealt with, there have been times when the victims ran out of money after maxing out credit cards and using up every available line of cash. The next step is often to borrow from friends or family. They might say they have a surefire business opportunity but are short on capital, or that they've come into a large amount of money but need funds to access it. Your father may have borrowed money intending to pay it back once he received his share of the fortune."

"So the guy gets mad because my father can't pay back the loan. But why the break-in?" she asked. "There's nothing to steal."

"It's possible that the break-in was merely intended as a form of 'encouragement' to pay up."

Goose bumps ran up her arms despite the warmth of the coffee she was drinking. "I don't want my father to know about the break-in."

"Lindsey." Kyle set his hands on the counter across from her while the onions sizzled, filling the room with their pungent smell. "How is that possible?"

"I don't know." She ran her fingers through her hair. "I'll replace the fish tank. The carpet people should be here any minute. I'll find someone to fix the window—"

"Don't you think your father should know about this?" He found a bowl and started whipping the eggs. "I think there have been enough secrets. He needs to know what's happened as a result of his actions."

"But the break-in might have nothing to do with Abraham Omah." Lindsey bit back the unexpected anger that swelled, feeling the need to defend her father despite his actions. "And even if it is connected, my father's not capable of dealing with this. But I am."

A smile registered on his profile. "You always were like that."

Her anger deflated like a collapsing balloon. "This still isn't your problem."

"You're determined to do this on your own, aren't you?" He folded his arms across his chest while the omelet cooked. "A man whose intentions were far from noble broke into this house last night. Your father's up to his ears in debt because this Omah guy is trying to take him for everything he's got. There are pending lawsuits against him. Shall I continue?"

She stared at the mug. She'd always taken on battles on her own. It allowed her to be in control. Giving situations over to God came hard enough. Trusting another person to help was almost impossible.

"You don't have to be a superwoman, Lindsey."

Why did his words always seem to pierce straight through her heart?

She held up her hand. "Okay. I hear you loud and clear. I'm not a superwoman. But I still want to fix this."

Kyle knew she was hurt. Confused. Angry. He knew because he'd been there before.

He decided to tell her the whole truth. "I didn't start my own securities business just because I saw a void in the market," he said, sliding half the omelet onto a plate and handing it to her.

She stabbed at her plate but didn't take a bite. "What do you mean?"

He combed his fingers through his hair. "We were talking last night about Michael."

"Yes."

"I didn't tell you everything," he admitted. "About six and a half years ago, he got involved in an Internet scam."

Kyle slid in beside her on one of the bar stools and took a bite of his omelet. He'd only told one other person—his business partner, Matt—the truth behind what had happened to his brother. Matt had been the one who'd told him flat-out to quit wallowing and get up and do something. Together they'd jumped into the financial-security arena headfirst, and Kyle had never looked back. Saving others from these disasters honored Michael's memory and helped ease the sting of his death.

"What happened?" Lindsey asked.

He pushed his breakfast toward the middle of the plate. "Michael was always special. You remember—he was a bit of a recluse and lacked social skills. He even struggled with depression once he started college. The demands were often too much for him. Still, everyone loved him."

"Yes, they did," she remembered.

"Six and a half years ago, he met a woman online. She was from Ukraine. Within a short time, he showed us photos of a beautiful woman and told us he was going to marry her. About three months into their online relationship, she asked him for three hundred and fifty dollars to pay for a visa to the States. The request seemed innocent at the time. She wanted to meet him in person. He was ecstatic. Next came the plea for an airline ticket. Michael was making pretty good money as a graphic designer so he agreed."

He noticed that Lindsey seemed to have forgotten her breakfast as she listened to him intently.

"Anya was due to arrive the day before Thanksgiving. I remember being genuinely happy that my brother had found someone. My mom went to so much trouble preparing all of Michael's favorite holiday dishes in honor of Anya's arrival. Yeast rolls, pecan pie and sweet-potato casserole. Michael had loved the holidays, and all the lights, music and food that went along with them. Dad even pulled out the Christmas decorations so we could decorate the house on the weekend. None of us had a clue what was about to happen."

"She didn't show up, did she," Lindsey said.

He shook his head. "Michael got a desperate e-mail saying that there had been an emergency. Her mother had fallen ill and had been rushed to the hospital with severe abdominal pain. Anya had no insurance and no money, and she needed twenty thousand dollars for an operation. Without the surgery her mother would be dead in a matter of days.

"Michael still lived at home and had saved quite a bit. I don't think he ever questioned whether everything she was telling him was legitimate. For him there was no other option. He loved her. He trusted her. Of course she was telling the truth."

By now their eggs were cold, but he didn't care. Dredging up these memories had doused his appetite.

"I remember asking Michael at one point how well he really knew her. But he wouldn't listen. He had photos. They'd chatted for hours online. He planned to marry her. How could I even suggest not helping her family? I backed off."

Guilt resurfaced. What would have happened if he'd done a background check on the woman? But he hadn't. Even after he began to suspect that Anya cared more about the Western Union deposits than his brother.

"Michael ended up wiring over forty-five thousand

dollars to the woman over the course of six months for hospital bills and physical therapy. Anya promised that as soon as her mother recovered, she'd come to America so they could be together. None of us knew what my brother had done until it was too late. His savings were wiped out, his credit cards were at their limit and he'd borrowed five thousand from a friend."

"And when the money ran out?"

"He never heard from her again." Kyle fought against anger that would never completely dissipate. Anger toward Anya, his brother's trusting nature and of course at himself for not recognizing just how deep Michael's depression had gone. "He overdosed on a bottle of prescription drugs. When we found him we rushed to the emergency room, but by then it was too late."

Lindsey reached out and squeezed his hand. "I can't imagine what that must have been like."

He stood up to reheat their eggs in the microwave. "I started doing research online and couldn't believe what I found. The statistics are terrifying and the scams endless. I discovered lottery scams, phishing and vishing scams, pump and dump scams. The truth is, if something sounds too good to be true, it probably is."

"Did the authorities ever find her?"

"She was just a faceless identity hiding behind a computer screen. We found a place to blacklist her name, but it's far too easy to come up with another identity before hitting up the next victim."

Lindsey's face paled. "Is it possible that we might never find the person who did this to my father?"

"We can notify the authorities but more than likely, they won't be able to do anything. It's extremely hard to track these criminals, even with good records and a lot of luck."

She took the reheated eggs from him. "There has to be a way."

"I do have a few tricks up my sleeve. I'll get a tech to scour your dad's computer for any electronic signatures that might help locate the perpetrator. But to be honest, Lindsey, in most cases victims never get their money back. What we have to concentrate on is keeping you and your father safe. Especially if last night's break-in was related."

She tucked a strand of hair behind her ear. "I'd say I'm pretty lucky you walked back into my life when you did."

"I don't believe in luck or coincidences." He smiled. "I'm taking you on as my first Dallas client. Pro bono."

"Kyle, no," she said, holding up a hand in protest. "You have a business to run. You'll go broke taking on pro bono cases."

"I'm not taking on a bunch of pro bono cases, I'm taking on one," he countered. "Besides, you won't find a better bargain this side of the Mississippi."

"Or on the other side for that matter." She cocked her head and held his gaze. "You're sure about this?"

"I've never been surer. Think of it this way, if you have to. Our firm is gathering intel on a certain Internet-scam ring and any additional information I get could potentially help take them down."

"I'll still owe you big-time. I'm sure my nonprofit salary doesn't come close to paying your invoices."

Her cell phone rang on the other side of the counter. She checked the caller ID and frowned. "It's my father."

"You're not in this alone anymore, Lindsey. Remember that."

She shot him a grateful glance and took the call.

# SEVEN

Lindsey couldn't shake the feeling someone was watching them. She pushed her sunglasses up the bridge of her nose and quickened her pace to match Kyle's long stride as they crossed the crowded parking lot toward the pet shop. She hadn't expected him to come with her, but when her father called to tell her that he was being released this afternoon, Kyle had insisted that he'd rather shop for a fish tank with her than sit cooped up in a hotel room waiting until his sister got home from a birthday party with his nieces. Lindsey had taken him at his word—she was glad he'd come along.

A bead of perspiration formed on her temple. Even before noon, the temperature was already well over ninety degrees. She glanced to her left. A tired-looking mom worked to get four kids inside her car. A Volkswagen bug parked in front of them, while a blue van drove past slowly, searching for an empty spot. Lindsey shook off the eerie sensation. These were Saturday-morning shoppers looking for a bargain, not burglars, stalkers and Internet scammers.

Still, the reality of the past few hours hung heavier

than the humid Texas air. On top of all that had been lost, the thought that the scammers didn't care what happened to the victims made her sick. But it was true. Abraham Omah wouldn't care that her father was lying in a hospital bed, just like Anya wouldn't have cared that Kyle's brother had died simply because he loved her.

She sidestepped a piece of bubble gum stuck to the hot pavement. Much of her father's behavior the past few months finally made sense. Guilt and worry had affected him both emotionally and physically, turning him into a recluse. If he'd only told her the truth from the beginning.

Tires squealed behind her. Music blared. Lindsey's heart thudded wildly. She slammed into Kyle, trying to get out of the way. Her knee hit the bumper of a parked car. Pain shot up her leg. The vehicle zoomed past, skidding toward the exit.

She watched them drive away. It was nothing more than a carful of teenagers on a joyride.

Kyle grasped her shoulders to keep her steady. "You okay?"

"Yeah." Her hands shook as she rubbed the sore spot on her knee.

"Just of bunch of rowdy kids looking for trouble." He pressed his arm around her shoulder. "Come on."

Unable to stop herself, she stole another look behind her. The blue van she'd noticed before was circling a second time. She peered into the tinted windows as it passed. The driver had his face turned away from her. Caucasian. Dark, longish hair. She shook her head. She was panicking over a man who was probably out looking for a special on tennis shoes or pet food. Last night's break-in had affected her more than she wanted to admit, but she refused to let the situation get the best of her. There had to be a way to fight back. To win.

And she would win, she told herself.

She stopped in front of the pet shop and took in a deep breath. "Ready to buy a fish tank?"

Kyle chuckled.

"What's so funny?" she asked.

"Back in college, I never would have imagined that one day we'd be shopping for a fish tank together."

She laughed, enjoying the sensation of a momentary stress release. The automatic doors slid open, blowing out a blast of air-conditioning.

"Lead the way," he said, letting her go in first.

She caught his boyish grin and felt a tingling sensation shoot to her toes. Somehow, Kyle Walker had managed to waltz back into her world and give her the only sense of stability she could find at the moment. If she weren't so worried about her dad, fish-tank shopping might have felt like a date—of sorts.

She spotted the tanks toward the back, past the half-dozen birdcages, food products and an outlandish display of designer doggy clothes and toys. The things people spent their money on amazed her.

"Lindsey?" said a familiar voice.

Halfway down the dog aisle, Mrs. Paden, one of her father's neighbors, stood holding a set of squeaky plush toys. No doubt another gift for the woman's prized twin boxers, Lulu and Mickey, who were notorious for chasing the neighborhood cats—especially Sammy.

Lindsey shoved her hands into the front pockets of her jeans. "Mrs. Paden. How are you?"

"I'm fine." The older woman's smile widened as her gaze traveled from Lindsey to Kyle. "Your father didn't tell me you had a boyfriend."

Mrs. Paden was as notorious for her candor as for her marauding boxers.

"A…boyfriend?" Lindsey stammered, feeling a blush creep up her cheeks. "No, this is Kyle Walker. He's an old friend in town for Sarah's wedding. Kyle, this is Mrs. Paden. She lives next door to my father."

"It's nice to meet you." Kyle shook the woman's hand, looking slightly awkward.

Mrs. Paden didn't seem to notice. "I'd forgotten Sarah was getting married."

"The wedding was last night," Lindsey said. "Kyle was the best man and I was the maid of honor."

Mrs. Paden's smile widened farther if that was possible. "You always make such a lovely bridesmaid."

"Thanks." Lindsey cringed, certain that her blush now matched the red, squeaky fire hydrant on the shelf beside her.

"Tell me, Lindsey, how is your father? I heard he'd been taken to the hospital."

Lindsey glanced at Kyle, thankful for the change of subject. She was certain that at this moment he'd rather be cooped up in his hotel room than continue this conversation with Mrs. Paden. "My father blacked out, fell and hit his head, so they wanted to keep him under observation for a while."

"Oh my." Mrs. Paden's smile faded. "I'm so sorry."

"The good news is that he called me a few minutes ago and said that he thinks the doctor will release him later today."

"What a relief." Mrs. Paden pressed her hand against her chest and then leaned forward as if she was about to reveal a dark secret. "I also heard about the break-in. It's frightening to think about where this world's headed, isn't it? We're not even safe in our own houses."

So much for keeping the attempted burglary a secret from her father. She'd forgotten how hard it was to keep a secret in the neighborhood. Add to that, the mixture of retirees and stay-at-home moms made it the perfect breeding ground for gossip. On the positive side, the sense of community had helped her worry less about her father. If he felt under the weather, one of the women was bound to show up at the door with a pot of soup or a casserole. Still, there were times—like now—when she wished word didn't spread quite so rapidly through the grapevine.

On the other hand, maybe she could turn the situation to her advantage.

"Did you see anything last night, Mrs. Paden? Around midnight?"

The gray-haired woman laid the set of animal-print bones she held back on the shelf. "Only what I told the police."

"Which was?" Lindsey prompted.

"A vehicle drove down the alley behind the house about that time. I thought it strange because normally it's so quiet at night. I was up getting a glass of water at the time and saw the van go by."

"A van?" Lindsey glanced outside. "Do you remember what color it was?"

"It was dark, so I couldn't say for sure. Blue, maybe black."

Lindsey's mouth went dry. No. It was only a coincidence. Nothing more. There had to be thousands of dark blue vans driving around Dallas.

"I keep complaining that there's nothing but a bare street lamp lighting our driveway," Mrs. Paden continued. "I've told my husband a dozen times that we need the city to install more lights. With crime escalating the way it is, one can't be too careful. Why, just the other day I was talking to Patty Loveland—she lives five doors down, you know—about how last week's paper recounted…"

Lindsey glanced at Kyle as Mrs. Paden droned on, and then cleared her throat. She had a lot to do if she was going to have her father's house ready before he returned home. "I'm sorry, Mrs. Paden. I'd love to stay and chat but I still have a couple of errands to run for my father."

"You tell him I'll be over in a day or two with a pot of his favorite soup."

Lindsey smiled. "I'll be sure to let him know."


Kyle stepped into the hospital elevator behind Lindsey and pushed the button for the sixth floor. In the space of a few hours, they'd managed to set up the new fish tank, complete with its colorful—still living—pair of African cichlids, and refile all her father's paperwork. The only sign remaining of last night's break-in was the shattered back window that would be replaced on Monday.

He glanced at Lindsey and saw worry on her face. He knew she was still thinking about that blue van—she was convinced it was following them. She'd seen it—or a similar vehicle—twice since the pet shop. Once on the freeway. A second time just outside the hospital parking lot.

While Kyle didn't want to dismiss her concerns, he had a hard time believing the connection was legitimate. Scammers didn't need people on the ground to do their dirty work. The Internet was their world. They could function from any country, under any name, with nothing more than a computer and a few generic e-mail accounts. No DNA or hard evidence left behind at a crime scene. That's what made them so elusive, so hard for the law to bring down. They didn't follow victims in dark vans and break in to their houses. Why should they when they could access their victims from the privacy of their own homes, or even in some Internet café halfway around the world?

No. The only plausible connection was if Mr. Taylor borrowed money to pay Omah and then accidentally ruffled someone's feathers when he didn't pay it back. But even that was a dubious scenario in his mind. More than likely the van was irrelevant and the break-in had been nothing more than a random burglary with very bad timing.

Lindsey leaned against the back wall of the elevator and stared at the floor. "I hate this. Trying to deal with some faceless criminal online is hard enough, but if they're right here—"

"You have enough to worry about, Lindsey. Don't drag in the possibility of that blue van being involved."

She glanced up at him. "It's possible, though, isn't it?"

"Just like it's possible someone put a bomb underneath this elevator."

She shot him a piercing glare. "Now, *that's* a comforting thought."

"Sorry. All I'm trying to say is, don't borrow trouble."

She gave him a half grin. "Are you reminding me once again to stop playing superwoman?"

"Ah. You're finally catching on."

The doors opened, and he followed her past the nurses' station toward room 617.

"Not only am I a slow learner at times, but it's always been hard for me to give situations over to God." Her sandals clicked on the tiled floor. "I'm very good at keeping at least a corner of the problem for myself."

He understood all too well what she was saying. "I admit to being a hands-on guy who wants to be in on every step of the process. That's why you found me working during Brad's wedding. A bad habit, to say the least."

"I'm glad I'm not the only one."

She stopped halfway down the hall. "I don't want to do this, Kyle. I'm about to confront my father about the fact that he's foolishly fallen for a scam and given his entire life savings away to some con man."

"You've got to understand that there's still a good chance he won't be ready to admit there's even a problem," Kyle said.

Lindsey cocked her head. "What do you mean?"

"He's so emotionally involved in the situation that he probably hasn't even admitted the truth to himself."

"He sold my mother's porcelain collection and went into debt."

"Exactly." How could he tell her that the situation

would probably get worse before it was over? "All he needs to know right now is that you will support him no matter what."

Closing her eyes, she took a deep breath. "You're right."

"Are you ready?" he asked.

"As ready as I'll ever be."

Kyle hung back as Lindsey greeted her dad, not certain how her father was going to react to his presence.

"Hey, Daddy." She leaned over and kissed him on the forehead. "They're letting you out today?"

"The sooner, the better. The food here is terrible. No salt, no sugar, no flavor."

She laughed and sat down beside him on the bed. "Daddy, do you remember Kyle Walker? We were friends back in college."

Kyle shook the older man's hand. "It's nice to meet you again, Mr. Taylor."

"Weren't you that math major who tutored Lindsey?"

Kyle nodded. "The one and only."

"Then if I remember correctly, I owe you a few thousand dollars. You saved Lindsey from having to repeat classes, and me from having to pay more tuition."

"Dad. I wasn't that bad."

Kyle laughed. "I'd say we can call it even. Your daughter had a rare talent for doing laundry that saved me a time or two."

"Why didn't you marry this guy, Lindsey? I like him. He's smart, funny—"

"Enough." Lindsey rolled her eyes. "What did the doctors say?"

"I have an infection, which apparently is common with the cancer, but I should live."

"Is the pain any better?"

"A little. At least my hip's not broken." He waved his hand in dismissal. "Enough of me. I need a good distraction. Tell me what you've been doing the past few years, Kyle."

Kyle glanced at Lindsey, wondering how much he should disclose up front. "I own my own business."

"Really? Well, that's quite impressive. What exactly do you do?"

Kyle paused. "I'm in…finances."

"He works with international-fraud cases and security issues," Lindsey threw in.

Apparently she had no problem getting straight to the point.

"Wait a minute, Lindsey." Her father's face paled as he tried to sit up. "Does this have to do with what we talked about this morning? Because if it does—"

"He can help, Daddy." She pressed her lips together, looking directly at her father.

*Don't crumble now, Lindsey. Your father needs you.*

"If I told you I don't need your help, then I certainly don't need his help," Mr. Taylor spouted. "You don't understand any of this. Either of you. I told you everything was fine. You have to trust me."

"Yes, but—"

"Lindsey, Abraham would never defraud me." Mr. Taylor's jaw tensed. "This is a private business matter. One I went into with my eyes wide open. Any losses I suffer are due to a corrupt foreign government. Not Abraham." He grasped his daughter's hand. "He's my friend, Lindsey. Not a criminal."

Except Abraham *was* a criminal. And even if her

father refused to admit it, he was worried. Kyle could tell by the older man's clenched jaw and the beads of perspiration on his forehead.

"Sir, I understand your hesitation in wanting to talk about the situation, especially to me. But you need to know that all we want is to ensure that you're not taken advantage of financially or in any other way, for that matter. We're worried that Abraham Omah—"

"I thought I made it clear that I don't need your help."

"You did make it clear, Daddy," Lindsey said. "But that doesn't take away the fact that there is a problem that can't be ignored. We know what happened. You gave Abraham everything you had saved. You sold Mom's porcelain figurines. You can't deny that."

Mr. Taylor shook his head. "I will not discuss this. Not now. Not ever. I told you to trust me."

"This isn't about trusting you," Lindsey said. "It about seeing the truth for what it is."

"Lindsey, I've always taken care of you and your mother financially and nothing has changed." His mouth tightened. "My business association with Mr. Omah is private."

"Daddy, I think you're wrong. You need to be concerned about Mr. Omah." She got up off the bed and stood beside the window that overlooked the city. "Kyle, please. Tell him what you've told me about these schemes."

Kyle looked at Lindsey's father. A vein pulsed in the older man's temple. As much as he wanted to help, the last thing he wanted to do was come between her and her father, or cause further strain on his health.

"And I don't want or need your services." Mr. Taylor looked at his daughter, shaking his head slowly. "I...I want..."

His words slurred. He pressed his hand against his chest.

"Daddy?" Lindsey crossed to him.

Her father didn't respond.

"Something's wrong," Lindsey said, panic in her voice.

Kyle ran into the hallway and called for help.

# EIGHT

Lindsey felt Kyle's hand on her elbow as the nurse asked them to stand back from the bed. The doctor entered the room. Lindsey fought to breathe. Her father's face was pale, his eyes closed. Sharp voices rose above his ragged breathing as they worked on him. If she lost him now…

Kyle pulled her toward the door. "You don't have to stay and watch—"

She shook her head. "I can't leave him."

Memories of her mother's death swept over her, filling her with grief. Why hadn't she waited at least until he was out of the hospital to confront him?

"Miss Taylor," the doctor said after five minutes that had seemed like an eternity.

Lindsey wrapped her arms around her waist. "Yes?"

"We'll be running some tests to confirm, but it looks as if your father had a TIA, which is a ministroke," the doctor told her. "The positive thing is that the symptoms don't last long, and, when treated, are completely reversible."

"So he's going to be all right?"

"There are two main things I'm concerned about right now. These ministrokes are often a precursor to a larger stroke, so we will be watching his vital signs closely." The doctor scribbled something on her father's chart. "The other issue is his infection, but I promise that we'll do all we can to ensure he has a complete recovery."

"Can I stay with him?"

"For a few minutes, but he needs to rest."

Kyle touched her shoulder. "I'll wait in the hallway."

Lindsey nodded and sat down beside her father on the bed. A bit of color had come back to his cheeks, and his breathing had returned to normal. "I thought I was going to lose you, Daddy."

His eyes opened and he shook his head. "I'm tougher…than I look."

"I know."

*I don't want this situation to consume either of us, God. You've got to show me what to do.*

She squeezed his hand. "I want you to know that I love you. I don't care what happened. We can forget about it or fight it—anything you want—but right now all I want is for you to get strong again."

One of the nurses stepped back into the room. "I'm sorry, but I'm going to have to ask you to leave. He needs to rest."

Lindsey kissed him on the forehead, then joined Kyle outside the room.

"You okay?" he asked.

"Yes…no." She shot him a half grin.

"Let me take you home now so you can rest. I know you're exhausted—"

"I can't. Not yet."

"Then what?"

Lindsey looked up at Kyle. "The answer to all of this has to be at his house."

Kyle punched the elevator button. "Then let's go."

Lindsey tried to shrug off the fatigue that had wrapped itself around her body. She needed caffeine. Desperately. She turned onto her father's street, making a mental list of the things she had to do. Making a pot of coffee was number one.

She stifled a yawn.

"You've been through a lot," Kyle said.

"All because of one man's greed."

Parking the car against the curb, she scanned the front yard. Everything looked the same as when she left earlier this morning. The eerie shadows from last night had disappeared beneath the bright, noonday sun. The hedge in front of the house had been recently clipped, and despite the dry weather, the lawn looked green. She followed Kyle up the sidewalk. Abraham Omah might have taken her father for a ride financially, but he wasn't going to ruin either of them. She would fix this. For her father.

She slid the key into the lock and pushed open the door. Her hand flew to her mouth.

Papers lay strewn across the floor beside CDs, coffee-table books and photos.

Whoever had broken in last night had returned.

She started to enter the house, but Kyle gripped her arm from behind. "Don't go inside. Let me make sure that whoever did this is gone."

He pulled out his phone and dialed 911. She stood frozen in place. The couch was tipped over, and the television lay on its side on the floor. The only thing still in place was the cichlids, swimming in their new tank.

After checking the rest of the house, Kyle was back beside her. "They're gone."

Her hand shook as she bent down to pick up what was left of the wooden clock.

The piece had no value other than the fact her mother had bought it on a whim one day they'd spent together garage sale shopping before she died. Beside an old coin collection and a few pieces of jewelry, there was little of value in the house.

"This has something to do with Abraham Omah, doesn't it?"

Kyle held a couple of CDs in his hand. "You're right, Lindsey. This wasn't a random burglary."

An hour later, the police left, leaving Lindsey to pick up the mess. Numbly, she rubbed the back of Sammy's neck. At least they hadn't hurt the cat. She fed him, then looked up at Kyle across the room. While she was thankful for his company, even he couldn't help with the tangle of emotions she felt. Anger, sadness, hopelessness—at the moment, the list seemed endless.

She picked up a picture of her and her mother off the carpet. The glass was fractured; the edge scratched. Running her finger across the photograph, she tried to remember the freedom she'd felt that day. Her father had snapped the candid shot beneath the Eiffel Tower two weeks before cancer took her mother. Before her father's depression led him straight into the path of an Internet fraudster.

"You okay?" Kyle set the couch upright, then started picking up a scattered stack of magazines.

"Yeah." She set the frame on the file cabinet beside another cracked photo. "As okay as I can be, considering the circumstances."

"We're going to get to the bottom of this."

She glanced around the room. It would take hours to put the place back together—and days to track down whoever did this. She had a few days of vacation saved up. She'd take the week off, spend time with her father and figure this whole thing out.

It was one thing to clean up the physical mess left behind, she thought. But trying to help her father heal emotionally was going to be a whole other story. She still had a hard time believing he had let this happen. Frugal and stingy, he'd traveled some, spoiled her mother at times and saved and invested. Looking around the living room was proof of that. The television, still on its side on the floor, was fifteen years old. The aged-leather recliner was even older. His favorite line had always been, "Why get a new one when the old one is perfectly fine?"

Regret swept over her. If she'd kept her mouth shut at the hospital, he might have been released this afternoon to come home. But to what? She grabbed on to the side of the couch to steady herself and fought to get her composure back as the room swirled around her.

"Lindsey." Kyle took her shoulders and set her down on the couch, sitting next to her. "At least your father's all right."

"I know," she said, sighing deeply. "But all of this is my fault. I never should have brought up the subject. He told me to trust him."

He tilted her chin so she had to look at him. His features blurred before her as she fought back tears. "You've got to understand something. Your father's in a lot of trouble. He's lost more than money—he's feeling shattered, vulnerable and embarrassed. No matter what you said to him today, he's had to deal with the situation and its consequences every day and that has taken its toll."

"I know." She hiccuped.

"This isn't your fault, Lindsey."

Her eyes widened. "You heard what the doctor said. A ministroke could be a precursor to another stroke. If he dies…"

"Listen to me. He's going to be okay," Kyle insisted. "Your father is a bright, educated man who loves you very much. Nothing that has happened changes those facts. That's what makes this so difficult for him."

"What do I do to help him?"

"Support him. Let him know you love him. And don't let him deny there's a problem. He's going to need you now more than ever."

She glanced across the living room. Sunlight poured through the sheer drapes that overlooked the manicured backyard. Four and a half years ago, she'd moved back in with her parents for six months to help care for her mother while she went through cancer treatments for the second time. Then her mother had died. She didn't want to lose her father as well.

She couldn't sit. "I need some coffee."

"Is that your solution to stress?"

"Yes." She went to the kitchen and filled the coffeepot with water, pouring it into the coffeemaker. "What did you do when you lost Michael?"

"I blamed myself and promised that I'd find a way to make sure his death wasn't for nothing."

"What about God?"

Kyle leaned against the counter. "I told Him it wasn't fair. Yelled at Him a lot. Even threatened to stop going to church."

She scooped her favorite cinnamon blend into the machine. "And did you?"

"No. God kept finding ways to remind me that He was in control."

Control. That was exactly what she'd just lost. And her life had ceased being so black and white. The answers seemed just out of reach. "But how do you turn over the whole situation to God and let Him handle everything? Because I'm not sure I can do that."

Kyle steepled his hands. "Honestly, I'm not sure I ever gave it to Him completely. There are still days I struggle. What happened to my brother still seems so wrong."

"Are you still angry at Anya?"

"Anya, my brother and even God some days."

She pulled open the kitchen blind and let the sun spill into the room. God's handiwork lay all around her. But sometimes even that wasn't enough.

*I need more faith, God. More of a grounded faith so that when things go wrong I know You are still there.*

Why did hard times always seem to come with doubt instead of a reassuring calmness that He really was in control?

The aroma of cinnamon filled the room as she grabbed two mugs from the cupboard. "How do you deal with the anger?"

"One day at a time, I guess. I have to let go of my

anger every day while I struggle with forgiveness, hatred and anger toward a woman I didn't even know. What I do know is that I don't want it to destroy me."

And neither did she.

The phone rang. Lindsey flinched. She was tired of jumping at every shadow and sound. She picked it up and pressed the receiver to her ear. "Taylor residence."

There was a short pause on the other end.

"Lindsey?"

"Yes? Who's this?"

"Vincent Lambert."

Lindsey tried to match the name and twangy Texas drawl with a face. Golf…that was it. Her dad's old golf buddy. Gray hair, slightly bald, late fifties…

"Mr. Lambert, of course." She forced a smile into her voice. "I'm sorry. It's been a long time."

"Yes, it has. If I remember correctly, the last time I saw you, you were getting ready to go back to school."

"Then it has been a while. I finally graduated about seven years ago." She pulled the milk out of the fridge and reached for the sugar bowl. "I guess you're looking for my father?"

"We were supposed to meet for breakfast out at ol' Jack's place this morning, but he never showed up. Got worried something might be wrong."

Lindsey took a deep breath. There was no getting away from the reminders. "I'm sorry. Dad was admitted to the hospital last night."

"The hospital? Is he okay?"

"I think he'll be fine. He blacked out yesterday and hit his head. Then this afternoon, he had a ministroke. They're running tests and keeping him for observation."

"Wow. I'm so sorry." There was a pause on the line. "If there is anything I can do…"

"Thanks." The coffee stopped dripping and she filled the mugs "I appreciate the offer. For now it's just a waiting game."

"That's too bad, because I wanted to invite him to a party I'm hosting next Thursday. A charity event at my house, though I suppose he's not going to be up and around by then."

"He should be home, but I doubt he'll be up to any socializing."

"I had hoped he might enjoy catching up with a few old friends. Well, in case you need a night out, you're welcome to come. It's black-tie and very snooty, but the food will be worth any trouble."

Lindsey laughed before taking a sip of her coffee. "Thank you for the invitation. I'll have to see how things go."

"I understand. Let him know I called, will you?"

"Certainly."

She hung up the phone. Kyle had left his coffee on the counter and was cleaning up the living room again.

"You don't have to do that."

"I will admit that it's a bit off my normal job description, but I don't mind." He'd almost filled an entire box with broken glass. "Who was that?"

"An old friend of my father's. He said they were supposed to meet for breakfast this morning, and then invited me to some swanky party he's throwing next week." She went to dig the vacuum cleaner out of the front closet. "I told him I'd have to wait and see, but I think I'll be too busy for socializing."

He set the TV upright on its stand. "I've run the scenario through my head a hundred times, Lindsey, but it always comes out the same. The break-in has to have something to do with money your father borrowed."

"A warning, you mean?" She crossed into the living room and surveyed the damage, shaking her head. "Two days ago I was worried about wearing some cheesy bridesmaid's dress, and thankful that my father's cancer prognosis looked good. Today, my father's lying in a hospital bed, and I don't know if I can forgive the man who did this to him."

"It's going to take time."

"But is it wrong for me to want to go after him and see him put away in jail for a very long time?"

"I don't think so. Considering your father isn't the only one Omah has scammed, catching him will make this world a better place."

She set her coffee down at her father's computer. "So as my newly 'hired' antiscam expert, what do we do?"

Kyle snatched his mug from the counter and took a sip. "Free e-mail addresses are nearly impossible to trace, so we start with the Western Union money transfers. If we're really lucky, we'll be able to track the beneficiary."

She grabbed some files off the floor and started trying to organize them. "That sounds like a good place to start. And after that?"

"The computer screen is cracked, but the hard drive looks okay. We can haul it down to the tech guy in my office and find out. If there's something there to find, he'll find it."

Lindsey smiled. "Then let's get to work."

# NINE

Lindsey dropped the last box of files onto the conference table in Kyle's new downtown office space, and then fell into one of the leather chairs. Good thing she'd decided to take a few days off. The job before her looked insurmountable. While his tech guy started on the computer in the other room, she and Kyle faced three boxes full of money transfers, e-mails and financial statements from the past year—plus the computer—from her father's house to Kyle's new downtown office space. She let out a sigh. There was no way out of it now. Her father was going to kill her.

Giving her power of attorney had been a concession to make life easier on her if something happened to him, but he'd made it clear it was only to be used in the case of an emergency. Still, who could argue that this wasn't an emergency? She might have broken every rule of privacy in the past twenty-four hours in her father's eyes, but between Abraham Omah's scam, threats of a lawsuit and now a house that looked like a war zone, even he could be made to see that she was doing the only acceptable thing.

Or so she hoped.

And she'd thought she could keep all of this from him. There was no getting around the fact that she'd have to tell him everything. Eventually.

Her purse teetered on the edge of the table. She shoved her father's mail into the side pocket, then set her bag against the wall, away from where they were going to work. She went to the window, rolled her shoulders and tried to relax. The view from the third floor revealed a bright blue sky overlooking a park.

Behind her, glass walls, a dozen sleek cubicles and simple artwork conveyed professionalism. She was definitely impressed.

Kyle walked into the office with two cups of steaming-hot coffee. He was catching on to what kept her going.

"Two cappuccinos with froth."

"Perfect. Thank you." She blew on the coffee and took a sip. "Your setup here is fantastic."

"You should have seen the place two weeks ago. I was convinced we'd never be able to open on time." He set his coffee down and started unpacking the first box. "You have to spend money to make money. Anyone willing to invest in our services expects us to know what we're talking about, but they also expect a certain atmosphere."

She took another sip. "This is no way to be spending your vacation, you know."

"It's a working vacation, and besides, do you hear me complaining?" He shot her a wide grin.

She smiled. She certainly wasn't complaining, either. At least she wasn't doing this alone. "So. Where do we start?"

"As I see it, we're looking for two things. First, the person your father borrowed money from. If we find anything that points to a suspicious transaction, let's set it aside. I'm hoping he'll soon tell us on his own but for now, keep your eyes open."

"And the second thing?"

"The second thing is a little harder. Besides looking for electronic signatures left on your father's computer, we need to try to trace the money to Abraham Omah."

"How?" Tracking down Internet scammers was a long way from working at a nonprofit organization, but she was a quick learner. Especially when the stakes were high.

"I need detailed lists of all the bank accounts your father sent money to, the names of beneficiaries and the ten-digit money-transfer control number off the Western Union receipts. Then we can start running the numbers through our computer database." He dumped a stack of e-mails on the table. "Needless to say, it's not an overnight process."

"That's pretty clear." She looked at the looming pile of papers and wondered what exactly she was getting into. It was great that her father had kept everything, but it meant that they were going to have to wade through all of it.

"The bottom line is that the scammers are professionals, and they don't want to be found. Their job is also fairly risk free as funds are typically dissipated through an extensive laundering process that's extremely difficult to track." Kyle took a sip of his coffee. "What we can do is search for key beneficiaries and signatories of the primary bank accounts, and work to identify their assets."

"Things like bank accounts and property they might own?" she offered.

"Exactly. Companies, nonprofit organizations… anything we can tie them to. If we get lucky, it will all link to a ring Interpol is already tracing."

Lindsey frowned. Knowing that an international police organization could be involved in her father's case seemed to further intensify the seriousness of the situation. On the other hand, the more people involved, the more likely they could get to the bottom of things. She started to work, praying that this would all pay off and help to bring down an entire scam ring. That would mean fewer scammers sitting behind computers—and fewer innocent people getting caught in their nets.

"And there's one more thing." He leaned against the edge of the table and shot her one of his don't-argue-with-me looks. "I don't want you staying at your place."

"What?" She quirked a brow.

"Just until we know what you're up against, I think it would be best if you stayed somewhere else. As a precaution."

Lindsey blinked. "Kyle, I don't think my life is in any danger. Whatever they want, I don't have."

"That might be true, but they don't know that. And from what we've seen today, this person is very determined to get what he's after."

She didn't like this. Her one-bedroom apartment might not be a palace, but it was home, and she didn't relish the thought of leaving.

"If something happens to you, who's going to take care of your father?"

She hated where Kyle's train of thought was going,

but even she had to admit he had a point. "I suppose I could stay with a friend."

Kyle drummed his fingers against the table. "I...I called my sister, and she said you're more than welcome to stay there."

Her eyes widened. "You what?"

"I'm sorry, but she's someone who can't easily be linked to you. I really think it's best. She told me it's no problem."

"I don't know." Lindsey hesitated. "There are complications."

"Like…"

"What if someone follows me there? I couldn't live with the fact that I put your sister and her family's lives in jeopardy—"

"That's a good point, but I've already talked to my sister about that. First of all, we can take extra precautions to ensure we're not followed. Secondly, my sister's house has a state-of-the-art alarm system."

Lindsey still wasn't convinced. "I'd still feel like an imposition. I haven't seen your sister in years, and—"

"You haven't seen me in years. Is my presence an imposition?"

Her heart tripped. "That's different, Kyle, and you know it."

"She's invited us for dinner at six."

"You're incorrigible."

"Thanks." He smiled at her and went back to sorting through papers.

Kyle felt his stomach growl. His sister, Kerrie's, husband was getting home late from playing golf, which meant dinner was late. The spicy aroma of homemade enchiladas filling the kitchen was torturing him as he unloaded Kerrie's dishwasher. His six-year-old twin nieces had roped Lindsey into teaching them a few tricks on the trampoline outside and his view from the kitchen window showed that she was good. Not that he was surprised.

"I always thought you should have dated Lindsey." His sister tugged at her ponytail, then went back to buttering the rolls. Thirteen months his junior, she'd never had a problem with being completely frank with him, and tonight was no exception. "She's perfect for you, you know."

He wiped a bowl and stuck it on the top shelf, avoiding her gaze. "We never exactly had a chance to find out."

"You mean you never took the chance."

"There were plenty of good reasons."

"What's stopping you now?" she countered.

"Kerrie…" He tried to come up with an excuse but couldn't.

"Now, don't tell me that dating her hasn't crossed your mind at least once during the past twenty-four hours."

"Nope." He shot her a wry grin. "It's crossed my mind at least a dozen."

She beamed. "I knew I was right."

"But now's not the time." He dried his hands on a dishcloth and wiped down the counter. How his sister always managed to rope him into helping in the kitchen, he had no idea. "Her father's in the hospital and we're trying to do the impossible by tracking down this Internet scammer—"

"So a man can't woo a girl because she's in trouble?" She smoothed down the bottom of her tank top and frowned. "What happened to knights in shining armor showing up to save the day? Sounds like the perfect fairy tale if you ask me."

"Maybe you've been reading too many of those to the girls," he retorted.

"And you've been spending too much time working. You should settle down."

Leave it to his sister—she didn't mince words, that was for sure.

The back door slammed. Lindsey stood in the doorway with a puzzled look on her face. How much of their conversation had she heard? Her cheeks were red, but he couldn't tell if it was from exercise or embarrassment.

She slid on her sandals. "Did I interrupt something?"

"No." Kyle wasn't about to give his sister a chance to interfere with Lindsey in the room.

Maybe his brilliant idea of keeping her safe at his sister's wasn't quite as ingenious as he'd first thought. On the other hand…he studied Lindsey's face. Rosy cheeks, clipped-up hair, wide smile. It was going to be hard to ignore his sister's candid advice.

The twins raced in from outside and grabbed Lindsey's hands, trying to pull her back outside.

"That's enough, now. Shut the door, girls," Kerrie said.

"I'd forgotten how much energy six-year-olds have," Lindsey said with a smile.

"Try two," Kerrie said.

Both women laughed. Kerrie shot him a knowing look. Boy, he was in trouble.

Kerrie wiped her hands on a towel, still smiling. "Simon called and is stuck in traffic, so I thought I'd give the girls a bath before we eat if the two of you don't mind."

"Of course not," Kyle said.

"The park behind us is beautiful. Why don't you take Lindsey for a walk, Kyle. It's cooled off enough to be pleasant."

Kyle grinned at Lindsey. There was no getting out of this. Not that he wanted to.

"I like your sister," Lindsey said once they'd started down the street.

"She's more of a mother than a sister, but I wouldn't trade her for anything."

Kerrie had been right about two things. One, the park was beautiful with its well-kept lawns and stately trees. Kids played on the jungle gym, while a Little League team practiced on the softball field. A mother pushed a baby carriage, joggers ran by…

Kyle glanced at Lindsey. Kerrie had been right about Lindsey, too. In college, he'd wavered between what majors to choose and what girl to ask out. Lindsey had been the uncomplicated, safe friend—for the most part.

Now he knew what he wanted, but the timing was all wrong. No woman had ever made him seriously consider settling down. Until now.

Kyle stopped. The open field blurred before him. Players ran. Fans cheered.

Maybe part of him had spent the past decade wishing for something he'd missed out on years ago.

"Kyle? You okay?"

"Sorry, I was just…" *Wondering what it would be like if we were together.* "Just enjoying the scenery."

*Coward.*

"I called the hospital about an hour ago," she told him as they started walking again. "They've moved my dad to a monitored bed, and he seems to be improving."

"That's good."

"Definitely."

"Any word on when he'll be able to come home?"

"He'll be in at least two or three more days. They didn't know for sure."

He could smell her perfume mingling with the scent of freshly cut grass. He looked at her, watching the breeze blow the strands of hair that had fallen from her clip. "You know, I was planning to ask you out that night."

She stopped and looked up at him. "What night?"

"The night you left to move back home."

Lindsey gnawed on her bottom lip. "The night I left you a note to say goodbye."

"Kind of kills a man's pride, getting a note like that."

"I never meant to hurt you." A shadow crossed her face. "My mom was sick, and my dad wasn't handling things well… I just left. I'm sorry."

"No, Lindsey." He shook his head and resisted reaching for her hand. "I never blamed you, and you certainly don't have to apologize." He cleared his throat. "I just… I guess I've always wondered what might have happened if I had asked you out."

"I always regretted losing track of you. You were a good friend, Kyle."

Friendship didn't sound as good as it used to. "You hungry?"

"For the first time today, yes."

"Kerrie makes a mean enchilada." He glanced at his watch. "Simon should be home in a few minutes."

"Then I suppose we should head back."

They gazed at each other for a moment, neither of them moving. Then Kyle's stomach growled and Lindsey couldn't help but laugh.

Still, something told him things would never quite be the same between them.

Lindsey fell back onto the couch beneath two squealing girls, her lungs burning for air from laughing so hard. She tickled Carly while Caileigh wiggled to pull off her shoe. There was a bonus to staying here—between playing with the twins and hearing a few amusing anecdotes about Kyle, she'd been able to forget what was happening. Kyle's family was the perfect distraction.

Her purse fell off the edge of the couch onto the carpet, spilling lip gloss, her father's mail and pens across the floor.

"Girls. I think it's time to settle down." Kerrie stooped to help.

"Don't worry about it," Lindsey assured her. "I've had such a great time tonight."

"Will you read us a story?" Carly asked.

Kerrie looked at the wall clock and then shook her head. "Not only is it way past your bedtime, little ladies, but I'm sure Miss Lindsey needs a breather."

"Tomorrow, girls. Okay?"

While the girls kissed their uncle good-night, she picked up her father's mail. She'd avoided looking at it all day, not wanting to face another letter from a collection agency. She was as bad as her father. She flipped over the top envelope. It was from the insurance company. Her father had taken out a policy years ago, though she had no idea what it was worth.

"How easy is it to cash in a life-insurance policy?"

Kyle looked up from the magazine he was reading. "It depends on what kind."

She tapped the letter against the palm of her hand. For a moment, she felt she shouldn't open it.

But then reality kicked in. If they were looking for large amounts of money, this letter could contain important information. She slid her finger across the flap then pulled out the letter. It was a personal note from her father's insurance agent. She scanned it quickly and dropped it into her lap.

"He canceled his policy last week, Kyle."

"How much was it worth?"

She shrugged. "I don't know. The letter just says thank you for your business, we're sorry to see you go."

He stacked the magazine back on the pile beside him. "Is there a number you could call to find out?"

She looked at the letter again. "Here. Max Banks. He's an old friend of Dad's—he included his cell number. Maybe he'll tell me something."

She flipped open her cell phone and punched in the numbers. He answered on the third ring.

"Mr. Banks, this is Lindsey Taylor, George Taylor's daughter."

"Lindsey. How are you?"

"I'm fine, thanks, though my father's in the hospital."

"I'm sorry. Is he going to be all right?"

"I think he'll be home in a few days." She rushed on with the reason for her call. "As you know, I have power of attorney for my father, and I need to ask you about something, if you have a moment. I just received the letter regarding his canceling his insurance policy."

"Oh, yes. I was sorry to lose your father's business. He's been a great customer all these years, but even I couldn't blame him for the deal he got on that boat. I say if you're going to retire, you might as well enjoy it."

"A boat?" Surely her father hadn't sold his life-insurance policy to buy some seaworthy vessel.

"Mahogany hull, twin diesel engines…" He let out a low whistle. "Your father had me wishing I could retire."

"A boat?" she repeated.

"You sound surprised." His voice cracked. "Don't tell me this was a surprise?"

"Honestly, I…" Lindsey didn't know how to respond.

"He got the check, didn't he? We mailed it to him early last week."

"I don't know, to be honest." Her chest began to constrict. "Could you tell me exactly how much money the policy was worth?"

There was a short pause on the line. "Just over sixty-five thousand dollars."

# TEN

*Sixty-five thousand dollars.*

Lindsey tried to focus on the lively discussion about II Corinthians 4 currently under way in the singles' Sunday-school class at her church, but she couldn't shake that dollar amount. Or the dozens of questions flying around in her mind. She scribbled down the questions in the notebook she kept in her Bible for taking sermon notes. Why had her father canceled the policy? Had he cashed the check? If so, what had he done with the money? And why didn't he trust her enough to talk to her about it?

Her temples pounded. She pressed her fingertips against her forehead and massaged, trying to alleviate the pain. Sixty-five thousand dollars couldn't vanish into thin air. And there were only four options she could think of. She made another column on the page and started a bulleted list. One: Her father still had the check. Two: He'd cashed the check and stashed the money somewhere. Three: He'd wired the money to Abraham Omah, though so far they hadn't found a corresponding Western Union receipt. Or four: He'd paid the money to someone he'd borrowed from.

But if the last option were true, who had he borrowed from?

She tapped the pen against the paper, wishing that the answers would come as easily as the questions. Sixty-five thousand dollars was a lot of money. That much money could have supplied plenty of motivation to whoever broke in to her father's house. She shook her head. It seemed that the more she tried to understand what her father was up against, the more daunting the reality became.

She stole a peek at Kyle, sitting beside her with his Bible open, obviously interested in the topic. She suddenly felt very unspiritual. Coming to church today had been a concession. She'd rather have been at the hospital interrogating her father—the only thing that stopped her was the doctor's strict orders that he rest. So she'd accepted Kyle's offer to bring her to church. But listening to a lesson, no matter how good it might be, was the last thing she felt like doing. Not that she blamed God for this situation—at least not completely. She mainly blamed herself for not seeing what was going on before her father had dived headfirst into this bottomless pit.

Kyle nudged her with his elbow. She flipped her notebook shut, shooting him a guilty look. She hadn't heard a single word for at least thirty minutes.

"This is good stuff," he whispered.

"I know." She leaned back against the folding chair. "I can't concentrate."

She forced her mind back to the Apostle Paul's encouragement in II Corinthians, currently being read out loud by Bryan, their teacher. "'We are hard-pressed on every side, but not crushed, perplexed, but not in despair—'"

Crushed and perplexed. Throw in the despair and that was exactly what she was feeling at the moment. She opened her Bible to the passage. Verse sixteen caught her eye. *Therefore we do not lose heart.*

Right. Don't lose heart. How in the world was she supposed to do that? She flipped her notebook open and stared at her scrawled observations. Despite Abraham Omah, a ransacked house and the missing sixty-five thousand dollars, the Bible was telling her not to lose heart. And that wasn't all. Paul clearly said that in spite of being hard-pressed and perplexed we were *not* crushed.

Or in despair.

She blinked back tears. *Then why do I feel so desperate, God?*

She glanced around the class. Two-dozen familiar faces filled the room. Some were friends she often had dinner with after the Sunday-night service. She'd joined the softball team, participated in local outreaches and even enjoyed singing with several of them on the chorus. Yet there were few—if any—she'd ever bared her soul to.

Taking in a deep breath through her nose, she tried to relax. Somehow she had to get through today without falling apart. The last thing she wanted to do was make a scene. And bursting into tears in the middle of church would definitely qualify as a scene. It might be biblical to share a burden with others, but it was much easier to keep the family soap opera to herself.

She focused on Bryan's words, determined to get something out of today's lesson.

"Verse eighteen," he was saying, "reminds us to fix our eyes not on what is seen but what is unseen."

Ouch. She was definitely looking at the temporary. Lost money, lawsuits, Internet scammers… As difficult as the situation might be, if her eyes were fixed on heaven, she'd also be thinking of the steady rock she had in her Heavenly Father. Yes, there was temporary pain and consequences of her father's actions, but whether he had a million dollars in the bank or a debt of a million, did it really matter? In the end, all that mattered was that their relationship with God was right, that she forgave her father—and herself—and that she didn't allow hatred toward one man to plant bitterness in her heart. The end of verse eighteen said it all. What is seen is temporary. What is unseen is eternal.

*I know you're speaking to me, Lord. I'm just finding it so hard to deal with the mess my father's made.*

A heartfelt prayer by one of the members brought the lesson to a close, but did little to rein in Lindsey's battered emotions.

"I really liked the class," Kyle told her as she gathered her things.

Before she could respond, several friends approached them, wanting to meet Kyle. She breathed a sigh of relief when they made it through the conversation without anyone teasing her about bringing a date to church.

The foyer was packed with people filing into the sanctuary for the morning service. Lindsey felt a lump in her throat and she pulled Kyle aside. "I don't think I can go in there."

He touched her arm. "Don't you think this is what you need most right now, Lindsey? Time with God, worshiping with your spiritual family?"

"Yes, but—"

She felt a light tap on her shoulder. Mrs. James, one of the leaders' wives, stood beside her wearing one of her signature hats—a red number with three plump roses on one side.

"I just heard your father was in the hospital, sweetie." Concern registered in the older woman's gaze. "How is he?"

Lindsey adjusted her purse on her shoulder. "The doctor believes he suffered a ministroke yesterday, but thankfully the symptoms are temporary. They think he'll make a full recovery."

"That's good to hear. I have to say, I've been worried about him for quite some time." Mrs. James leaned in closer. "He used to be so involved in church activities, but lately he's dropped out of sight. My Henry's been by to check on him several times, but he never wants to talk."

Kyle shot Lindsey a pointed glance.

"You know, Mrs. James, my father is going through a really difficult time. I don't feel that I can divulge any details right now, but the situation is very serious. I'm doing everything I can to help him, but honestly, he really needs the church's prayers."

"God knows the details, sweetie." The older woman's reassuring pat brought with it a reminder that God was in control—Lindsey didn't have to do this on her own. "Promise you'll let us know if there's anything specific we can do. That's what we're here for."

She hesitated briefly, wondering how her father would feel about visitors. She decided they'd be good for him. "He'll be in the hospital a few more days. He might appreciate a visit."

"Consider it done."

"Now, that wasn't so hard, was it?" Kyle asked as the older woman walked away.

Lindsey let out a soft laugh. "I guess not."

"What do you want to do now?"

Praise music began in the sanctuary and a wave of peace washed over her. "Let's go inside."


"You're looking better than you were yesterday, Daddy." The praise service had lifted Lindsey's spirits more than she'd anticipated, giving her the necessary emotional energy to talk to her father.

He sipped water through a straw. "The pain in my hip is still intense, but I am feeling better."

Color had returned to his face, and the monitors tracking his heart showed a steady beat and only slightly elevated blood pressure. All symptoms of the stroke had vanished. The challenge now was getting the information she needed without upsetting him.

She set her purse on the floor and settled back in the chair. Kyle had brought her but insisted he wait in the lobby. Finding out the truth, he'd told her, would be easier if he weren't around.

She wasn't sure her father would tell her anything, regardless of whether Kyle were there or not. She'd have to start slowly. "A lot of people missed you at church today. They're concerned. Mrs. James told me she was planning to drop by to see you.

Her father fiddled with the IV line on his arm, avoiding her gaze. "I know you want answers, Lindsey, and I know all of this is confusing for you."

"All I want is what is best for you."

He pressed his lips together but didn't say anything more.

"Daddy, I don't like meddling in your personal matters, but I am worried."

He looked at her, frowning. "I told you—I need you to trust me, Lindsey."

She studied the monitor. His heartbeat remained steady. It was now or never.

"Can I be completely honest with you, Daddy?"

"You know you can." His words sounded amiable but he set his jaw and looked away.

She sent up a short prayer for wisdom and took the plunge. "I talked to your insurance agent yesterday. He told me you canceled your life-insurance policy."

"Lindsey—"

"Daddy, please. I can't ignore what's going on. Surely you can understand that."

She glanced at the monitor—his heart rate went up slightly.

"I'll admit to making a bad investment or two. I ended up having to borrow some money."

"And that's why you cashed in the life insurance?"

He nodded.

Good. They were making progress.

"Was the money to pay Abraham or someone else?"

His eyes narrowed. "I don't want you involved."

She wanted to tell him about the two break-ins but she was afraid he might shut down completely—or worse. How could she make him understand she needed answers? And that she was on his side?

"Daddy, I already am involved. At least tell me who you borrowed money from."

He shook his head. "The less you know, the better."

"How are you doing, Mr. Taylor?" A petite redhead in blue scrubs walked in, chart in hand.

"Not much has changed since you checked on me fifteen minutes ago."

"Your father has a stubborn streak," the nurse told Lindsey.

Now, *that* was an understatement.

"So does my daughter."

Lindsey laughed, but the bleak reality of the situation had stolen any real joy from her voice.

Her father yawned. "I need to sleep."

She ignored the nurse's nod of agreement. "Changing the subject?" Lindsey asked him.

"Yes."

"We'll talk later." She leaned down to kiss him on the forehead.

"Promise me you'll leave the situation alone?"

"Have a good rest, Daddy," she said, leaving the room.

Kyle stood outside the hospital, while he waited for Matt to answer the phone. Home from church by now, his friend was either taking a Sunday-afternoon nap or watching baseball. More than likely, the latter. Matt liked baseball, apple pie and a certain blue-eyed brunette named Megan he'd met last month. Time would tell if this relationship made it past the one-month mark.

He suddenly realized that his track record wasn't much better.

Matt picked up just before the phone switched to voice mail.

"Matt. Hey. How are things in D.C.?"

"Don't tell me you're calling on a Sunday to ask about work. Hang on a second—let me mute this." The baseball game in the background went silent. "Are there problems with the new opening?"

"No. Not at all. We'll be up and running tomorrow."

"That's what I want to hear. I knew there was a reason that I agreed to be your partner. So what's up then?"

Kyle hesitated, knowing what Matt's reaction was going to be. He might as well jump in and tell him straight. "I took on a new client."

"Great."

"Pro bono," he added.

It took a full four seconds for what he'd said to sink in.

"Wait a minute. Aren't you supposed to be on vacation this weekend? Why are you spending time finding ways to suck money from our vast empire?"

Kyle laughed. Someone had been watching way too much sci-fi lately. "Did I mention she has honey-blond hair, big brown eyes and—"

"In other words she's a knockout."

Kyle hesitated. Oh, yeah. Lindsey was a knockout. But the truth was, his reason for getting involved with her father's case went far beyond her looks.

"Actually," Kyle began, "she's an old friend from college I want to help."

"An old friend? Right. Tell me more."

"All I'm going to say is that she's smart and nice—"

"Smart and nice? How many years have I known you? I can read between the lines."

Kyle combed his fingers through his hair and smiled.

Man. Matt knew him too well. And how did he always manage to box himself into a corner? "Save it for another day. That's not why I called."

Matt chuckled. "I'll back off for now, but it's about time you found someone. She's interested, right? I bet she is. Even I know you're not a completely bad catch."

"Thanks a lot. How's Megan?"

Matt laughed at Kyle's change of subject. "I'm afraid she's too perfect for me. It's never going to work. Okay, back to the case. Give me the details."

"We've got a 419 scammer that's taken close to two hundred thousand dollars from Lindsey's father. And what's really interesting is, I'm seeing a lot of similarities between the scammer's signature and the guys we've been after. I'm still waiting for the preliminary feedback, but there definitely seems to be a connection."

Matt let out a low whistle. "Bringing down that ring would be worth any pro bono fees. Forward what you've got and I'll do some digging. We're going to get this guy."

"You got it." Kyle flipped his phone shut as Lindsey came out of the hospital. "That was my partner, Matt. He's going to do what he can on his side."

"Thanks."

"You're welcome." He tried to read her expression. "How's your father?"

"Stubborn. He refuses to give me any more information. He insists that he doesn't want me involved."

"I told you how common his reaction is. Admitting the truth means admitting that he's just fallen victim to one of the worst scams of the century."

Lindsey's head jerked up as a blue van approached.

"Kyle." Almost dropping her purse, she dug quickly

for a pen. Repeating the license-plate number out loud, she scribbled it on the palm of her hand.

Kyle studied the man's profile as he passed. Dark, long hair and a sharp nose. The driver pulled out of the parking lot onto the main road and sped away.

Lindsey's fingers gripped his arm. "That's the same guy, Kyle. He *is* following us."

# ELEVEN

Lindsey nursed a mug of coffee at the kitchen table, hoping the caffeine would help wake her up. Despite the comfortable bed in Simon and Kerrie's extra room, she'd slept horribly, disturbed by a recurring dream of running down a dimly lit street, away from the man in the blue van. She'd finally gotten out of bed to pray and think more about her father—sleep clearly not in the cards.

Kerrie, in cropped pants and a tank top, pulled a dozen blueberry muffins from the oven, their tangy fragrance spilling into the room. Lindsey marveled at how Kerrie had managed to make her feel completely at home, which was no small feat after everything that Lindsey had been through.

"You must have worn the girls out last night." Kerrie's bubbly laugh filled the room as she set the hot pan on the stove. "They rarely sleep past seven."

Lindsey yawned, wishing she'd been able to sleep in like the twins. She forced a smile. "I don't have any nieces or nephews, so I enjoyed playing with them. They're sweet girls."

Kerrie put the muffins on a plate and set them on the table in front of Lindsey. "You know you're welcome to hang around here as long as you need to."

"I appreciate that." Lindsey glanced at her watch. "As soon as the bank opens in a few minutes, I need to call them. I've got to see if they have any record of that insurance check."

"Scary, isn't it?"

"It is. Especially considering my father won't talk, and I'm not sure how much more I can do without his help. He thinks he's trying to protect me, but I feel like there's a noose tightening around my neck."

Kerrie slid the butter across the table. "I guess Kyle told you what happened to our brother, Michael."

"He did, and I'm so sorry." Lindsey stared at the muffins, trying to decide if she could eat. The past couple days had pretty much doused her appetite. "He was always so sweet."

"We all felt guilty after he died, but I learned one thing I'll never forget." Kerrie turned around and caught Lindsey's gaze. "'If onlys' eat you up inside and destroy you."

Lindsey frowned. Hadn't she been playing that very same game the past few days? If only she'd taken her father's withdrawal from life more seriously. If only she'd noticed what he'd been doing on the computer. If only she'd asked more questions.

Kerrie sat down at the table beside her. "The bottom line is that this is your father's life. I know how important you feel it is for him to tell you what's going on, but don't let his actions destroy you. Love him and help him all you can, but in the end, you can't change the past. And you can't force him to cooperate with you. Michael became just as stubborn about guarding his life. I think the embarrassment of what had happened turned out to be more than he could handle."

Lindsey mulled over the advice. "But my dad's life could be at stake. I can't just sit back and do nothing."

"Of course not, and that's not what I'm saying." Kerrie rested her elbows on the table. "Just do what you can, but don't beat yourself up in the process."

Lindsey combed both hands through her hair and tried to shake the wave of frustration threatening to pull her under. "I just wish it wasn't so complicated. I don't know what I'd be doing right now without Kyle."

Kerrie's face brightened and she leaned forward. "He's a great guy."

Lindsey smiled. Any guy who would jump headfirst into a situation like this had a heart of gold. That definitely described Kyle. She took another sip of coffee. Even though a long-distance relationship wasn't an ideal situation, it was becoming far too easy to picture herself and Kyle living in some quiet suburb with two kids in tow.

She grabbed the knife and buttered one of the muffins, popping a bite into her mouth. Kerrie slid back into the chair across from her, looking as if she was waiting for a response.

"So?"

"Kyle *is* a great guy." She took another bite of her muffin. That was easy enough for her to admit.

"And?

Boy, the woman just didn't give up. Lindsey searched for what to say. "I guess it's another thing I'm trying to take one day at a time. I certainly didn't expect him to come back into my life like he did, but now that he's in it…I don't know."

Maybe when things with her father were ironed out she could contemplate the two of them together. In the meantime, her father required all her focus.

Carly and Caileigh bounced into the room with more energy than Tigger, saving her from having to say any more. If only she could harness some of their energy, she'd be good to go. Lindsey greeted the girls with big hugs and kisses, thankful that they'd welcomed her into the family so joyfully.

Kerrie settled the girls in at the table with muffins and juice, and then nodded toward the glass French doors at the front of the house. "The bank's probably open now if you want to call. You're welcome to use Simon's office."

Lindsey promised the girls that she'd be back in a few minutes and slipped out of the room. Inside the orderly office, she sat at the wide mahogany table, tapping her fingers as she waited for the bank manager to pick up his phone.

"Eugene Watson speaking."

"Mr. Watson, this is Lindsey Taylor calling in regards to my father, George Taylor."

"Miss Taylor, I'm glad you called." There was a pause on the line. She could tell something wasn't right. "Since you've got power of attorney, there are some things I need to discuss with you regarding your father," he continued. "If you could come down to the branch this morning, I'd prefer to talk to you in person."

Lindsey glanced at her watch, uneasiness growing in the pit of her stomach. "I'll be there in twenty minutes."

Lindsey pulled her car into an empty parking spot in front of the bank, shut off the motor, then glanced at Kyle. Fear of discovering what her father had done was overshadowed by the fact that the sooner she found out the truth, the sooner she could put all this behind her.

Kyle touched her shoulder. "You ready to go in?"

She nodded. Sitting in the parking lot wouldn't get them the answers they needed.

Eugene Watson met them in the plush lobby, then quickly escorted them to his cluttered office. Lindsey took the offered chair beside Kyle and clasped her hands tightly around the strap of her purse.

Mr. Watson sat across from them with steepled hands, his expression serious. He seemed as nervous as she was. She swallowed hard.

"I'm not sure how to handle this situation, Miss Taylor, but I feel an obligation to let you know what happened." Lines creased his forehead. "Your father's been a client of ours for over twenty years, and I'm very worried that he's fallen into something…unscrupulous."

"What happened?" she asked.

Mr. Watson set his glasses on the table in front of him and rubbed his eyes. "Your father came in last Wednesday with a check from his insurance agency that he wanted to cash. Not an entirely unusual transaction, but I've known your father for so many years that it struck me as odd that he wanted such a large amount of money. He told me it was for a yacht, but your father has always been a bit…well…"

"Miserly?" Lindsey threw out. There was no use mincing words at this point in the game.

"Exactly. So you can understand how his cashing a check for over sixty-five thousand dollars to buy a luxury item stood out as anything but ordinary."

The timeline was beginning to come together. Her father had raised money from a source to pay Abraham. The deal didn't go through, which meant he couldn't pay back the lender. Thus the cashed life insurance.

"So he came in and cashed the check on Wednesday?" Lindsey continued her questions.

Mr. Watson nodded. "Originally that was his plan, I believe."

"Originally?" Lindsey shook her head. "I don't understand."

"As a longtime friend, I felt obligated to advise your father on the risks of carrying around such a large amount of cash. I suggested we transfer the money into his account instead of letting him leave the building with a briefcase full of cash."

"But he didn't go for that?"

"No. And something else bothered me as well. It might be nothing, but there was a man loitering in the lobby that morning. I eventually had one of our security guards ask him to leave when it became clear he wasn't here on bank business."

"He was following Mr. Taylor?" Kyle asked.

"I don't know for certain. But I decided to tell your father that the bank needed forty-eight hours to put the papers into order for such a large cash transaction. He wasn't happy, but he agreed to come back when the money was ready. I had hoped that this would give him time to reconsider, but two days later, he walked out of the building with the money."

*Sixty-five thousand dollars in cash.*

But where was the money now?

"The man you noticed the first time my father came in—did he return the second time?" Lindsey asked.

"I never saw him again."

Kyle leaned forward. "Have you got surveillance tapes? There's always the chance that Lindsey might recognize the man."

She squeezed her eyes shut for a moment and pinched the bridge of her nose. This whole thing was crazy. She was contemplating going through the bank's surveillance tapes in hopes of tracking down a criminal? She was a caseworker at an adoption agency, not a detective.

Mr. Watson tapped his glasses against the desk. "Our tech man is out today, but I could arrange for you to see the tape tomorrow, if you like. Anytime after, say, eleven o'clock."

"Lindsey?"

She nodded at Kyle. Wishing she could make it all go away wouldn't change anything. "That'll be fine. Thank you for your time, Mr. Watson."

"I wish there was more I could do." He stood to shake their hands. "I always liked your father and hated to think that someone might be taking advantage of him."

"Unfortunately, Mr. Watson, that's exactly what has happened, so I appreciate your help." Lindsey slung her purse over her shoulder.

"I'm sorry to hear that. If there is anything I can do, please don't hesitate to call."

* * *

Kyle stood in front of his sister's house, wishing he were coming to pick up Lindsey for a date. At least he'd managed to scrounge up a bit of good news for her along with a bag of tacos for dinner. In the space of the few hours that had passed since their meeting with Mr. Watson, he'd managed to have a meeting with clients, ensure everything was going smoothly on the first official day at the Dallas office and run those license-plate numbers. They still had a long way to go, but it was a step in the right direction.

"Hey." She stood in the doorway, smiling at him and making him wish he were spending his time getting to know exactly what he'd missed over the last thirteen years or so.

"Hey, yourself."

"Something smells wonderful." She looked rested and almost relaxed. Apparently she'd taken his advice and slept for a bit after spending the afternoon cleaning up her father's house with friends from church.

He held up the bag and waved it in front of her. "Mexican."

"How'd you know that's my very favorite?"

"I seem to remember a girl who could never turn down a trip to the local Tex-Mex diner."

"You're good if you can remember that." She laughed as he followed her into the house.

It was quiet, a rare occurrence at his sister's home.

"Where is everybody?"

"Kerrie took the twins to the mall for new shoes and pizza, since you said you were bringing me dinner. They'll be back in a little while."

He set the food on the kitchen table then grabbed a couple plates, smiling at his sister's obvious attempt to make this somewhat of a date. Lindsey pulled out two cans of soda from the fridge and handed him one.

"I ran the plates on the blue van and came up with a name."

Her eyes widened. "What's the name?"

"Do you know a Jamie McDonald?"

She popped open the can and shook her head. "Doesn't sound familiar at all. Does he have a record?"

"Nothing more than a few misdemeanors and speeding tickets."

"Can we find him?"

He took a swig of his soda. "I'll see if I can figure out who he works for and what he does. Maybe we can connect him to your father."

He'd wanted to have more for her. But any lead they came up with was a victory.

Her cell phone rang, and she flipped it open to take the call. Kyle watched as her brow furrowed. After a brief conversation, she hung up the phone and grabbed her purse.

"What's wrong, Lindsey?"

"That was the hospital. Someone phoned my father, and now they can't calm him down."

Kyle felt the knot in his stomach tighten. "Omah?"

"They don't know. All he will tell them is that it's an emergency." She wrapped her fingers around the strap of her purse and caught Kyle's gaze. "If he doesn't calm down the doctor's afraid he's going to have another stroke."

# TWELVE

The emergency, as her father had emphatically declared the night before, had to do with an impounded car. The black, two-door Mustang her father had been driving since the late 1980s. Her father had refused to say anything regarding the incident, other than to make her promise that she'd pick up the car and park it in his garage.

"I don't understand him at all." Lindsey stood beside the car in the impound lot and shoved a strand of hair behind her ear. "Why didn't he tell me this before? He was out when he collapsed, and his car was parked on the street. I thought he was home when it happened."

Kyle folded his arms across his chest. "I suppose your father deserves some leeway considering all that he's been through the past few days."

"I agree, but what was he doing the night he called 911?"

Lindsey frowned.

Something must have upset him enough to affect him physically. Had he met with Jamie McDonald? Had Jamie threatened that he had to pay up or else? Had the stress caused him to black out?

The questions were getting old. She wanted answers.

The only positive thing was that the car didn't look any worse for wear after being impounded and left in a dirty, packed lot for a few days. On the phone, her father had insisted she look it over carefully for any scratches or dents, but in all honesty, she'd rather drive away and leave the car at this dump. How many years had she been begging her father to buy a new model? He just insisted there was nothing wrong with driving the old one.

She handed her driver's license to the gum-chewing clerk, followed by a check for the pricey amount due, then signed on the dotted line. Her father would have owed her big-time if it weren't for the fact that he didn't seem to have a dime left to his name. How many more unpaid bills would come her way? She wanted to help him—she'd do anything for him—but she had no intentions of going bankrupt because of Abraham Omah.

"Can you tell me where the vehicle was picked up?" Lindsey took her receipt and slid it into her wallet.

The bored woman flipped slowly through a stack of papers. "Looks like it was brought in from downtown."

"Thanks."

Her father lived ten miles away. What business did he have downtown? Her hand grasped the set of extra car keys until they bit into her palm. She'd had enough of her father's secrecy. She was going back to the hospital and her dad was going to talk, no matter how embarrassed or ashamed he was. There were too many questions that had to be answered.

Kyle was waiting beside her father's car. She waved her hand at the offending vehicle. "There she is in all her glory. Her name is Betsy. I learned to drive in that car. I even took road trips to California and went to a few drive-in movies in it."

"Reminds me of my first car, except it was bright red." A quirky smile settled on his face as he ran his fingers across the hood. "I can understand your dad's obsession. If I hadn't totaled mine when I was eighteen, I'd probably still be driving it."

"You're kidding, right?"

"Not at all. I loved that car." He leaned against the frame and held out his hand for the keys. "And I'd be more than happy to drive it to your dad's house for you."

"Now wait a minute. Don't go getting all sentimental on me." She couldn't help but laugh. What was it with men and their toys? "My father would have a fit if I let you drive Betsy—she's like his second child. No one is allowed to drive her unless it's an emergency. I can promise you that the very thought of a stranger towing his car is driving him crazy right now."

"Please." The twinkle in his eye brightened. "This is a classic, and one I'm sure I appreciate far more than you."

"You're pathetic." She tossed him the keys.

Kyle caught them midair. "It worked, didn't it?"

"You're just lucky I trust you." She pointed at him. "Not a scratch."

Lindsey leaned against the driver's door. "How could my father have forgotten to tell me he'd left his car downtown?"

Kyle's playful grin faded. "I think his forgetting about the car is in line with everything else he's been through."

"Maybe." She brushed a leaf from the hood. "What if for some reason he simply didn't want to tell me?"

"More of his I'm-going-to-handle-this-by-myself attitude?"

"Exactly. We're assuming Dad still had the money Friday. But if he'd gone to meet with Jamie to pay him off, then why is the man following me? And why the break-ins? It doesn't make sense. He obviously didn't find what he was after. And where is the money now?"

"There are a hundred possibilities." Kyle leaned against the car next to her. "Maybe Jamie never showed up. Or your father might have left the money somewhere, deciding not to give it to him for whatever reason. There is even the chance that Jamie might be in on all this in an entirely different way. One we don't even know about yet."

Lindsey felt as if they were grasping at straws. She felt like bursting into the hospital and screaming at her dad to talk to her. Instead, she stared at a chip in her red fingernail polish. "I keep thinking about your brother, Michael. What made him cut you off when he needed you most? He had to have known how much you loved him."

"I've asked myself that question a million times." Pain crossed his face. "I'd always thought we were close, and that he knew that I'd be there for him no matter what. Anya changed all that. He never would admit she'd scammed him. It's the same with your father. We're looking at a very powerful combination. Pride and a bit of stubbornness."

"A bit?"

His grin came back. "Okay. A lot. From what I've

seen, your dad's stubborn enough to hold on to that naive belief that he can still somehow work this out on his own without affecting you."

"And get us both killed in the meantime. Sixty-five thousand dollars isn't pocket change. Someone wants it."

Kyle wrapped his hand around hers and pulled her against him. "I'm not going to let anything happen to you. I can be just as determined and stubborn as your father, Lindsey."

She buried her head in his chest. His heart beat steadily against her. Part of her wanted to stop and find out what she felt for this modern knight who'd ridden in on his gallant horse to help her. But for the moment, her father loomed between them. "I'm still scared of what this is doing to him, Kyle. To his future."

"One day at a time is all you can do for now. We'll get the answers."

She looked up at him. Tears filled her eyes, but she blinked them back. She wasn't going to break down again. "So what's the next step?"

"We need to find the money."

She nodded in agreement. "I think it's time we searched my father's house—thoroughly."

Lindsey shoved the shoe box into her father's closet and sighed. She'd found nothing other than old letters, his collection of Texas Ranger baseball hats and a box of suspenders. The clothes—items he'd bought over two decades ago—hung neatly on the wooden rack, but there was no sign of the money. The only thing their search confirmed was that he never got rid of anything and rarely bought anything new.

"Anything yet?" Kyle poked his head in the doorway of the master bedroom.

She shrugged, holding up a pile of shoehorns. "There's nothing much here but shoes, suspenders and socks. What about you?"

He shook his head. "Expired coupons, boxes of *Reader's Digest* and dozens of plastic grocery bags. But no money."

She stood to stretch her legs. An hour of searching in all the places the burglar hadn't touched had turned up nothing. Maybe he had sent the money to Abraham. Just because they didn't have a receipt through Western Union didn't mean he hadn't made the transaction somehow.

She folded her arms across her chest, mentally checking off all the places they'd searched. "We've pretty much looked everywhere."

"It might not be here, Lindsey."

She picked up a photo of her parents off the lace-covered dresser. Something had died in her father when her mother passed away. The spark of life that used to be in his eye—the love for travel and even Saturday afternoons fishing with his buddies—all seemed to have been buried with her.

His stubbornness, on the other hand, seemed healthier than a wild hydrangea. A visit to the hospital on the way to his house had been as unproductive as usual, though he seemed relieved about his car. But other than that, he continued to insist that he could—and would—handle things on his own and that Abraham Omah was a friend who had never attempted to defraud him. And nothing she could say would change his mind.

Rather than beat her head against the wall, she'd

walked out. He had always been stubborn, but this time his obstinacy came with a high price. Kyle's insistence that her father's behavior wasn't uncommon—that her father saw the situation as some fairy tale he was convinced would end happily ever after—did little to appease her.

"Where do you want to look next?" he asked.

Stretching her arms behind her head, she shrugged. She'd gone through the closet twice with no results. All that was left to search was the spare room. After that they'd be back to square one.

She searched the guest-bedroom closet while he searched the antique dresser her mother had bought at an auction. She reached to check the top shelf, and her hand hit something.

"Kyle, look at this." She lugged a box from the top shelf of the closet and set it on the bed. "This is a brand-new laptop."

He pulled out the computer, still in its plastic wrapper.

Lindsey plopped down on the blue-and-white comforter. "I can't imagine my dad buying this for himself. Not when he has a perfectly good computer in the other room."

"I don't think he did." Kyle sat down beside her. "Gifts are common. Computers, gold pens, cell phones. The way the scammers are able to pull their victim along is unbelievable."

She was tired of the tears that seemed to automatically spring to her eyes. It was like racing down the drop of an unending roller coaster and not being able to catch her breath. "I need a break, Kyle."

She stomped into the kitchen, fighting the urge to

scream. She needed a distraction. Opening the refrigerator, she pulled out a package of ready-to-make chocolate-chip cookies and turned on the oven.

"What are you doing?" Kyle entered the kitchen behind her.

"Baking. Thankfully, my dad has a sweet tooth," she said, holding up the cookie dough.

"Baking?"

He probably thought she was nuts, heading to the kitchen every time she couldn't handle something. "I don't know, Kyle. I think I'm calling it quits. You can go back to your own life and pretend none of this ever happened."

"You can't fire me."

"Oh, yeah? I just did."

Her head began to pound. She knew she couldn't just walk away from all of this, but for the moment, refusing to keep up the crazy detective charade felt good. And maybe she'd watched too many police dramas, but she was tired of worrying that someone was about to burst through the back door any second. Or that some guy driving a blue van would do something more than simply follow her. She was no super woman, clearly. She just wanted her life back.

She peeled off the plastic wrapper and laid the dough on a cutting board. "This isn't worth your time. It's not worth my time for that matter. My father's being impossible, the money's vanished, some crazy man's stalking me…" She threw up her hands in defeat. "I'm done with all of this."

He moved in beside her. "Be angry, Lindsey. Scream and kick those cabinets if you have to, but don't let that anger defeat you. You know you can't quit now. Your father needs you. Along with every other man and woman who's been taken in by these guys. Don't let them win."

She grabbed a serrated knife from the drawer, wishing he hadn't begun his valiant monologue. It just seemed like every time she managed to gather her courage, waves of doubts and fears would hit, and then she had to start over again from scratch.

She was sick of going from denial to anger and back. It felt far too much like the grieving process she'd gone through during her mother's illness and death. She had lost something then. And she'd lost something now, as well. She'd lost the father who used to take her to the park when she was five. Who used to make sure her dates brought her home by curfew. Who taught her how to stand up for herself when Mac Roberts had tried to bully her in school.

She started to slice the cookies. One after the next, in exactly the same size. At the moment, it seemed that slicing cookies equally was about the only thing she could control in her life.

She laid the last cookie on the sheet and shoved the batch into the oven. "Do you ever feel like all your expectations in life were foolish?"

He sat near her on one of the bar stools. "What do you mean?"

"My dad was always my hero." She leaned against the counter, eyes closed, as dozens of memories filtered through her mind. She wanted things to be like they were when her mom was alive. When she'd had a shoulder to cry on. Maybe that was the problem. The roles of parent and child had suddenly reversed, and she didn't feel ready to take on that responsibility yet.

She squeezed her arms around her waist. "My dad worked hard to provide for my mom and me, and he was good at what he did. He was smart, outgoing, and he was always there for me and my mom. He loved her so much. But now…"

"He still is that person, Lindsey."

"No, he's not." She opened her eyes. "That's the problem. He's not the person I grew up with, and it scares me. I don't want things to change. He's my father. He's the person I lean on when life throws me a curveball, and the one who helps clean up the mess when I make a mistake. The one who's always there for me."

"And I want Michael back alive. But no matter how much I want that, I'll never be able to turn back the clock. But there is something that hasn't changed."

"What's that?"

"Even if you have to start playing the role of provider for your father, he still loves you. More than anything. That hasn't—nor will it—change."

She pressed her hands against the counter and shook her head. "I'm sorry. It just hurts."

"There's nothing to be sorry about, Lindsey. It's an emotional process you will have to go through. You might never have the same relationship with your father that you once had, but don't let that erase all the good things from the past."

She stood in front of the stove, watching the cookies through the oven window. He was right. As usual, he seemed to have an answer. He'd been in the same situation she found herself in right now and he understood what she was wrestling with. It gave her comfort.

Sammy rubbed against her legs, crying as though

he'd been thoroughly neglected. "Did I forget about you, Sammy?"

Lindsey glanced at the cat's bowl. The water was still half-full, but the bowl was empty. A quick check of the cupboard revealed that she was out of cat food.

"Should I run to the store?" Kyle offered, his hands shoved in his front pockets. She could tell he wanted to do something to help take the load off.

"I don't think so. Let me check the garage. Dad normally keeps the extra cans of cat food out there."

As she made her way out to the garage, she chastised herself for being so emotional. Kyle was already helping her with her father—he didn't have to provide emotional support, too. Though of course he had been all along.

She found the food on the second shelf of the pantry. Exactly where she knew she'd find it. Her leg brushed against the fender of her dad's car as she headed for the door.

She stopped and turned around. The car. They'd checked everywhere but the car. Her father had been driving around Friday night. What if he had been going to meet someone? What if the money had been in the car when he'd been rushed to the hospital?

"Kyle?" she called out.

"Yeah?" He appeared in the doorway, the light from the living room shining behind him.

She started to open the driver's door, then stopped. She couldn't imagine her father walking away from sixty-five thousand dollars, no matter how sick he was.

"You think the money might be in the car?" Kyle asked.

"If Dad left the money in the car and knew it was

sitting out on some deserted street, do you think he would have told me?"

"Given the way he's been acting, no, I don't. I definitely think it's worth a look."

They checked the glove compartment, behind the seats, and the trunk.

Nothing.

Lindsey ripped through the glove compartment again, even looking for a hidden compartment or a fake panel. The money simply wasn't in the car.

"It's gone. That's all there is to it." She slammed the door shut, leaning back against it.

Kyle was staring into the trunk.

She walked around to the back of the vehicle. "Did you find something?"

"I thought it was empty, but…"

She followed his gaze. "The spare tire?"

Kyle lifted the tire. Nestled beneath was a bag of hundred-dollar bills.

# THIRTEEN

Kyle picked up a stack of hundreds and slipped out one of the bills. He held it up to the light and studied the head of Benjamin Franklin. It stood out slightly on the paper, unlike on a lifeless and flat counterfeit. The bordered edges were clear and distinct; the serial numbers the same color as the treasury seal. This was definitely the real thing.

He did a quick calculation, certain this was the missing insurance money—and the reason behind the break-ins. Instinct told him that Jamie was after this money, but he wasn't the lender. His boss probably was.

It seemed pretty obvious that whoever Mr. Taylor had managed to involve himself with wasn't the kind of person who handed out long extensions with his loans. Someone wanted this sixty-five thousand dollars, and they wanted it now.

If they could just figure out who Jamie worked for, they'd be halfway there. At least with one part of the problem. Abraham Omah was a whole other issue.

Lindsey stood quietly beside him, her knuckles white as she gripped the edge of the trunk. She picked up a stack and fanned through the bills. "He's blown his entire retirement, maxed out his credit cards, and now he has the gall to trade in the only remaining financial security he has without telling me? And it's not like he took the money for some legitimate reason. That I might understand."

"Lindsey—"

"And to make things even worse," she continued, seeming not to hear him, "he didn't tell me his car was out there on some deserted Dallas street—with sixty-five thousand dollars inside—bound to be towed. Sixty-five thousand dollars, Kyle. I mean, come on. The least he could have done was told me to get the car off the road and the money back in the bank, but no. He has to be stubborn and not tell me because of his so-called pride."

Kyle closed his mouth and listened to her frustrated ranting. He remembered several passionate monologues he'd delivered after Michael's death. Anger, irritation, fury. They were unfortunately all a part of the process.

The buzzer from the oven sounded in the other room.

She jerked her head in the direction of the kitchen and started moving toward the door. "The cookies are going to burn."

"Wait a minute." He tugged gently on her arm and pulled her back beside him. "Take a few deep breaths. I'll get them for you."

"What am I supposed to do with all this money?"

He picked up a duffel bag off a shelf. "Why don't you put it in here and we'll take it to the bank when we go to watch the surveillance video."

She grabbed the bag and started stuffing the piles inside.

The buzzer continued to echo across the house. Kyle headed for the kitchen. Embarrassment, shame and pride. They were all reasons why people refused to tell their families. George Taylor had fallen into the same trap Kyle's clients had fallen into dozens of times. But blame was never the answer. Action was.

He found a pot holder in the third drawer and pulled the cookies from the oven. In his line of work he'd seen more than his share of heartache, and every case made him more committed to stopping these scammers. While the elderly weren't the only people liable to fall victim, he'd seen the scenario played out over and over with older folks. George Taylor's generation had nest eggs and good credit to tap into. They'd been taught to be respectful and trusting, and were unlikely to report the fraud because of embarrassment. These were only a few of the characteristics that had caused Lindsey's father to play right into the hands of Abraham Omah.

Lindsey stomped into the house, slamming the garage door behind her. She dumped the duffel bag and can of cat food onto the counter. "I'm still furious, but some of this is beginning to make sense in a weird kind of way."

"How's that?"

She folded her arms across her chest, staring at the bag. "If something upset Dad enough, he could have passed out from the stress."

Kyle nodded. The contents of the duffel bag would be enough to send anyone's blood pressure through the roof. "If he was driving around with all that cash in his trunk, sick that he'd just cashed in his insurance policy, that's definitely enough to set in motion a physical breakdown."

"He must have parked the car and walked around while he decided what to do."

"Or maybe he was supposed to meet someone. Then at some point he passed out, hit his head and managed to call 911. Your father's lucky to be alive."

"I know." Goose bumps rose on her arm as she touched the money in the bag. "Have you ever seen so much money?"

"More, once."

She looked up. "How much?"

"It was a suitcase of cash. One hundred and seventy-five thousand dollars."

She let out a low whistle. "You're kidding."

"Nope. It was a setup to take down a group of scammers back in D.C. about three years ago. Eight were eventually arrested in the operation. It was one of those times when I wouldn't trade my job for anything."

She glanced up at him. "We're going to get these guys, Kyle."

"Now, that's the attitude I need to hear from you," he said, smiling.

She grabbed a spatula and started setting the cookies on a cooling rack, licking a gooey blob of chocolate off her finger. He felt a rush of emotion as he watched her.

*God, only You can bring something good from all of this.*

And he knew God would. How many times had he seen it happen in his own life? In his own church family? Tragedy struck and the road was rocky and often grueling, but in the end, hope always managed to spring up and life went on.

It seemed too pat to think everything would be all

right. But for the moment, clinging to hope was the best option they had.

Sammy rubbed up against his legs. Lindsey zipped up the money bag and opened a can of cat food. "Seeing all this money makes me want to hamstring the guy myself. My father didn't work his entire life to end up in the poorhouse."

"Are you ready to go to the bank?" he asked.

"Yeah. let's go see who is on that tape."

Lindsey shook the network administrator's hand. Tom Barter was short, wiry and suffered either from allergies or a horrid cold. He probably should have stayed home either way, but she was glad he'd come in. Another day of delays was the last thing she wanted at the moment.

"It's nice to meet you both." Mr. Barter pulled out a wad of tissue from his front pocket. He blew his nose as he motioned for them to follow him to an office in the back corner of the bank. "You're in luck. A year ago we were using a black-and-white analog system that was grainy and took days to sort through. In other words, it was pretty worthless. But the bank invested in a bit of up-to-date technology and voilà—you want a clear photo of this guy, I'll get it for you."

Lindsey followed him into the room with Kyle behind her. "We really appreciate your help, Mr. Barter."

She breathed a sigh of relief. The insurance money was now safe, back in the bank's vault where it belonged. But that was only part of the visit's objective. They had to find out who was so determined to get their hands on the money.

"This is my surveillance room," Tom said, sliding into his chair in front of the computer screen. "This system can pack an amazing punch. Two months ago, a guy tried to rob the place. In less than fifteen minutes, I had his photo and description off to the police. They caught him two days later."

Lindsey took a seat. "That's got to deter any would-be bank robbers."

"So you'd think." The man frowned. "There is the occasional smart aleck who thinks no one will notice him. Caught a guy pocketing a handful of credit cards from one of our manager's desks just last week. It's amazing what people will try."

Lindsey smiled, trying not to show her impatience. The talkative tech guy wasn't getting them there any faster, despite his fancy new system.

"Let's give this a try." Mr. Barter flexed his fingers above the computer keyboard. "The manager told me we're looking between ten and ten-thirty last Wednesday morning."

"That sounds about right."

"Okay. Then we'll set the time navigation. Source is the lobby…" He sneezed, then blew his nose again.

Lindsey shot a glance at Kyle. Maybe waiting another day wouldn't have hurt.

"You'll love this digital monitoring," he continued in his nasally voice. "The resolution will make you drool."

She sincerely hoped not. At least the man was enthusiastic about his job.

Lindsey studied the computer screen. The camera scanned the lobby. She picked up her father right away. He'd worn jeans and a polo shirt and he looked nervous.

She studied the footage, watching as he kept glancing behind him while he waited in line.

Something had definitely been wrong. But what?

She leaned in to the screen, looking for anyone who seemed familiar. A woman stood in line ahead of her father, one hand holding a little girl with pigtails while the other maneuvered a stroller with an infant. Two college-age girls chatted one line over. An elderly woman holding a shopping bag stood behind them.

Where was the guy the manager had seen?

A minute passed. Lindsey forced her eyes to focus. Kyle cleared his throat beside her. Mr. Barter blew his nose. Again.

And then a man appeared at the edge of the screen. Caucasian. Dark, long hair and a sharp nose. Her heart seemed to stop beating.

"That's him." Lindsey pointed to the top left corner of the screen.

Mr. Barter enlarged the frame. "Who is it?"

"Jamie McDonald. The man who's been following me."

# FOURTEEN

Lindsey drummed her fingers against the armrest of Kyle's two-door rental car, thankful that this time he was the one driving. Seeing Jamie McDonald standing behind her father in the bank line had shattered her nerves. Was McDonald working for someone? How far was he willing to go to get the money back?

"Are you sure you want to do this?"

"What choice do I have?"

It was time to lay her cards on the table and tell her father everything. She'd prayed about it. Even played out scenario after scenario until her head pounded from the effort. She knew she had to do it.

She'd called the hospital to check on his progress. His speech was fine. There was no paralysis. The nurses' frequent neurological assessments showed him at almost back to normal. After another day or two of observation, they planned to send him home.

She grasped the leather armrest as Kyle turned into the hospital parking lot, fighting off second thoughts. The last thing she wanted to do was cause a stroke. But as she'd told Kyle, what choice did she really have?

She'd tell him about the two break-ins, the money in the spare tire and Jamie. She knew that if anything would get him to talk, it would be concern for her. Knowing her life could be in danger would convince him that they couldn't play games anymore. It had to.

Kyle pulled into the covered entrance of the hospital and stopped in front of the glass doors. He looked at her, concern obvious in his gaze. "Lindsey?"

"I'm okay." She let out a deep breath and tried to relax—an impossibility the past few days. "You know you should be enjoying your vacation, or even working, for that matter."

He shot her a wry grin. "We're not starting this conversation again, are we?"

She laughed. "No."

"Tell you what. If you don't mind, I will go in to work for an hour or so. There are a couple of issues I'd like to deal with in person. Will that give you enough time?"

"Plenty. I plan to ease into the conversation as painlessly as I can."

"You'll do fine." He reached out and squeezed her hand. "Would you like me to pray?"

"Yeah. I'd appreciate that."

She held on to his words as he prayed. The soothing timber of his voice and his calm helped her relax slightly. When he was finished, she added her own silent request. *Please, God. I need my father to listen to me.*

She kept praying across the lobby, up the elevator and down the long, narrow hallway into her father's room.

"Hey, pumpkin. How are you doing?"

"I'm good." She reached down to kiss him on the cheek. He looked one hundred percent better. His color was back and his upper left eyelid no longer drooped. "The question, though, is how are you?"

"Ready to go home."

She set her purse on the narrow rolling table beside the bed and settled into a vinyl chair. "I thought you might say that. The nurse said you're doing better."

"The ringing in my ears is gone as well as the blurred vision." He reached out and squeezed her hand. Another good sign. "I'm okay. Really."

"And your hip?"

"The pain is almost gone." He reached for a glass of water that sat beside her purse. "I am sorry for all that has happened the past few days. It wasn't your fault I got so upset. I know you were only trying to help. I just…I don't want you to worry. Everything will be fine."

She shook her head. "Your house was broken into, Daddy—"

"What?"

She clasped her hands together, irritated at the unsubtle way she'd brought up the subject. Why couldn't she have reined in her emotions and dealt with this situation using common sense and a bit of tact? She'd wanted to. Planned to. But the entire situation made her too frustrated.

She glanced at the monitor. His heartbeat was still steady. "I don't want to upset you again. If—"

"Wait a minute." He pushed himself up to a sitting position. "What are you talking about, Lindsey? What happened?"

She swallowed hard, trying to figure out where to

start. The break-in? The sixty-five thousand dollars? Jamie McDonald? She decided to start at the beginning with the attempted break-in, and finish with Jamie McDonald on the surveillance tape.

By the time she was done, his eyes were wide with horror. "If anything happened to you, I'd never forgive myself."

"I'm fine, Daddy. Really."

"Have you called the police?"

"They've been out to the house. Twice. And Kyle convinced me to stay with his sister, just in case they decided to come looking at my house."

Her father shook his head. "You should have told me about the break-ins when they happened, Lindsey."

"I tried. You had a stroke."

"If you'd told me about the break-ins, I would have listened."

She leaned forward and caught his gaze. "How was I supposed to convince you that something was wrong when you decided to go into business with a complete stranger, sell all of Mom's figurines, cash in your life-insurance policy and invest your entire retirement in some…some…"

*Some Internet scam.*

Her stomach roiled. She couldn't bring herself to say the words out loud.

"I guess I can see how you might worry about Abraham." He fumbled with the pillow behind him, his brow beaded with dots of perspiration. "I didn't know him. I never really understood where he got my name."

Lindsey paused. Was he admitting that at least he suspected he'd never see any money from Mr. Omah?

"It's all related, isn't it? The life-insurance check. The money in the spare tire. Jamie McDonald."

He stared out the window, nodding. A pigeon perched on the windowsill, its iridescent gray-and-purple feathers shining in the early-afternoon sun. The bird flapped its wings and flew away. Her father watched as if he wished he could fly away and leave all this behind. She could certainly understand the feeling.

"I cashed in the life-insurance policy because I needed the money to pay back what I'd borrowed to pay Abraham," he finally admitted.

Except for the steady pulse of the heart monitor and a voice drifting in from outside, the room became quiet.

But she wasn't ready to stop yet. "So you borrowed money to pay Abraham and then when Abraham didn't pay up, you were stuck with another debt?"

"I don't owe Abraham anything. It's a slam-dunk business deal. And he will give me my share." His jaw tightened in anger. "Lawyer fees. Absentee-collector fees. Tax fees. You wouldn't believe these government officials we're dealing with. Every time we take a step forward they slap us with these ridiculous fees."

Lindsey swallowed hard. "And it's never crossed your mind that Abraham might be pocketing those fees?"

"How could you even think that? How can you continue to insist that Abraham is some low-class crook?"

*Because he is!*

His pulse quickened on the monitor and Lindsey knew she had to back off, away from Abraham, on to a hopefully less painful question. "What about McDonald?" she prodded carefully. "How'd you meet him?"

"McDonald met me at the bank to pick up the money.

That was it. There was nothing sinister about the situation at all."

"Except when he decided to get the cash on his own."

"You don't have any proof that Jamie was responsible for the break-ins, so you can't blame him. It could easily be a coincidence. Crime is up." Her father sounded if he was trying to convince himself as much as her. "Besides, he was just doing his job."

"Who does Jamie work for, Daddy?"

Her father avoided her gaze. "You worry too much."

"So that's it. Just like with Abraham, it's still none of my business."

"All Abraham asked me to do was let him transfer money into my account so his corrupt government didn't confiscate it. Since when is that a crime?"

"He took your life savings, Daddy."

He continued staring at the bed, avoiding her gaze. "All I've ever wanted was to make sure you were okay. To take care of you, and your mother before she died. I…I thought I could fix what was wrong with her. You have to believe that, pumpkin. And now…if anything were to happen to you…"

Lindsey's heart was breaking as he confessed. "Mama dying wasn't your fault."

"All we needed was a few more months." He clawed at the sheet, pulling it into a wrinkled ball between his fingers. "There were other alternative treatments that might have worked."

"No, Daddy. It was her time. God was ready to take her home. And she was ready to go."

Lindsey shook her head, wishing her father could let go of the heavy guilt he'd carried with him since her mother's death. He had done everything he could for her mother. No one could fault him on that. He'd loved her for forty years. Letting go was hard. But how could she get him to understand that in order to go on with his life that was exactly what he had to do? Let go of her. Not forget her—neither of them would ever do that. But the spiral of depression her death had triggered was dangerous. For both of them.

She tried to justify her father's actions. Sometimes forgiving oneself was harder than forgiving someone else. Did he really blame himself for his mother's death? Why? Because he hadn't been able to do enough? Because he hadn't been able to save her?

Kyle had blamed himself for his brother's death. She'd blamed herself for not discovering the mess her father had gotten into before he'd sent Abraham that first dime. But the truth was, neither of them could change the past. No one could.

So where did she go from here?

"Where's the money, Lindsey?"

Her father's question yanked her away from her thoughts. She blinked. "The money?"

"The insurance money." The gentleness in his voice had faded.

"Back in the bank where it belongs."

He shook his head. "I have to give Jamie the money."

"And what about Abraham?"

"I'll worry about that. I told you I would."

Tears filled her eyes. They were going in circles again.

She pushed herself up from the chair—she had to get away for a minute before she said something she'd regret. "I'll be back."

She escaped into the bathroom and pushed the large wooden door shut behind her. Bracing her hands against the sink, she stared into the bathroom mirror. Her mother's eyes looked back at her. Brown with dark rims. Long lashes. Strong, yet vulnerable at times.

*God, I miss her, too. So much.*

She missed her sense of humor. Missed her sage advice. Missed eating dinner together as a family, and playing board games past midnight until none of them could stay awake.

If only this were a three-hour game of Monopoly where she could pay fifty dollars to get out of jail, or pass go to collect two hundred dollars. But it wasn't. She didn't know anything about this game. Except that she didn't want to play anymore.

Kyle worked to focus on his laptop's screen. With today's stringent liability laws, if something went wrong, the corporation and its stockholders could be harmed. Which was a situation to be avoided at all costs. The bottom line was that there could be no mistakes in his work. His full evaluations included in-depth research and cross-references far beyond the scope of Google. And it all had to be done not only discreetly, but within the boundaries of privacy laws. That's why he'd spent the past ten-plus years ensuring he knew the science of due diligence and contract language like the back of his hand.

But the words on his screen kept blurring together because all he could see clearly at the moment was Lindsey.

Closing his eyes only made her image sharper. This

was a habit he was going to have to break if he was ever going to get any work done. Although he wasn't so sure he wanted to break it.

She'd looked up at him when he'd dropped her off at the hospital. Chin set at a determined angle. Lips pressed together like a soldier marching off to war. He'd wanted to play hero in that moment, scooping her up in his arms and tell her to forget everything that had happened the past few days.

Yep. He was falling for her. Hard.

*Wait a minute.* He'd worked long and hard to ensure that his company could outperform the competition—he couldn't now turn around and make a fatal mistake because a pretty girl had walked into his life. Not that he didn't want a wife and a home someday, but he tended to look at life efficiently, logically. There wasn't room for a wife and a home right now. But there was Lindsey.

He rolled his chair back from the table he was using as a desk and grabbed his coffee cup from the counter behind him. He took a sip. Ugh. Lukewarm.

His cell phone rang. He picked it up on the second ring. Caller ID identified his partner was checking in.

"Hey, Matt."

"You sound distracted."

"Just took a sip of cold coffee."

"Yuck."

"That's what I thought." Matt couldn't pass by a gourmet coffee shop without stopping. He understood the disappointment of cold coffee.

"Any holes in the report I sent you?" Matt asked.

"Not yet." Kyle didn't feel the need to mention he'd

read the first page a dozen times before processing a single word. Honey-colored hair was on his mind again. This really wasn't good.

"Then I'm already two for two, and it's not even lunchtime."

"Two for two?" Kyle said, confused.

"I think I found the connection between Jamie McDonald and Lindsey's father."

"Really?"

"Jamie McDonald works for Vincent Lambert, who just happened to serve with George Taylor in the same squadron some forty-odd years ago. It could be just a coincidence."

Kyle let out a low whistle. "I don't think so."

"So you know the guy?"

"No, but Lindsey's father does. And apparently they've stayed in touch throughout the years. Vincent called last Saturday morning, claiming they were supposed to have met for breakfast, but George never showed."

"Claiming?"

"The call sounded legit at the time, but with sixty-five grand at stake and a connection to Jamie, I'm beginning to have my doubts. More than likely, Jamie's nothing more than an errand boy for his boss."

"So what's the next step?"

Another piece of the puzzle had just fallen into place. "Listen to this. Vincent invited Lindsey to some charity event at his house tomorrow night."

"Looks as if you've just found the perfect setting to pull together a bit of firsthand info on the man."

Kyle smiled. His thoughts exactly. He couldn't remember the last time he'd looked forward to a job-related social event. Too bad he'd had to return his tux last weekend.

"Seems like Lindsey and I are going to a party tomorrow night."

# FIFTEEN

If it wasn't for the fact that they were at the Texas Liberty Charter School fund-raiser to scope out Vincent Lambert, Lindsey would have found the atmosphere perfect. Perfect enough to make her wish she could call this a date. But as romantic as the ambience might be, this was definitely not a date. Kyle looked fantastic though in his black tux. The guy really knew how to dress when the occasion called for it.

Little expense had been spared to turn the elaborate gardens into an elegant night for charity under the stars. A small band played music with a Latino beat in the background. Two long buffet tables, running along the covered stone patio, were laden with everything from quesadillas and carved roast beef and turkey, to colorful fruit bowls and mouthwatering cheesecake. The enormous, two-story house, located in a wealthy suburb of North Dallas, added to the stylish setting. Whatever Mr. Lambert did for a living, he must do it well.

Lindsey's stomach grumbled as she placed a couple of chocolate-covered strawberries on her full plate. She might as well enjoy herself while she was here. She added an irresistible slice of cheesecake and then focused on balancing her plate, drink and purse as she followed Kyle down a paved walkway toward one of the many tables. It wouldn't be completely dark for another couple of hours, but already strings of white lights lit up the patio and a dozen of the trees in the spacious backyard. Beyond the green lawns, a lake sparkled in the distance, its boat ramp adding even more value to the high-priced property.

Kyle chose one of the smaller tables for two at the far edge of the pool. They sat down, close enough to be able to observe the guests, but far away enough to ensure a bit of privacy. Which was exactly what she wanted at the moment. From here she could observe their host mingling with his guests while they decided on their game plan.

Her mouth watered as she bit into a juicy strawberry. "Tell me everything you know about Vincent Lambert."

Kyle grinned at her. "If I don't, will you dump cake on my shirt?"

"Ha-ha, very funny," she said, cringing at the memory of chocolate frosting on his white tuxedo shirt. "Come on."

"Okay. Here's what I found out about him. After graduating from high school, he went straight into the army and served four years in the same battalion as your father. When his time was up, instead of reenlisting, he moved to Dallas, where he married Rachel Prim and started working for his father's contracting company. Edward Lambert died six years later, leaving the entire business to him." Kyle glanced up from his notes. "Apparently, the man has a bit of the Midas touch. Anything he puts his hands on turns out a nice profit. Let's see." His gaze dropped back to the notebook. "Divorced ten years later with two kids still in elementary school. He married Priscilla Maxwell, with whom it's reported he'd been having an affair, but the marriage only lasted seven months."

"Now, that's really sad."

"I agree. Five years ago, he married his current wife, who happens to be fifteen years younger than him. She has a daughter from a previous marriage who is currently enrolled at Harvard."

"With stepdaddy picking up the bill?"

He flipped the notebook shut, then tapped on the cover. "That I don't know for sure, though it does seem likely."

"So, barring his failed marriages, he seems to be quite the model citizen." She waved her hand toward the dozens of partygoers who seemed to be enjoying themselves. "Including hosting charity events."

"I wouldn't go so far as to call him a model citizen." Kyle brushed the notebook against his leg. "Five years ago he was investigated for attempted fraud. Nothing was proved, so the case was dropped, but now there seems to be financial doom hovering on the horizon."

Lindsey leaned forward. "Really?"

"Most of what I found out were rumors, but some of them came from pretty trustworthy sources. Mr. Lambert seems to be losing his touch. About four months ago, he was sued and he lost. Since then, he's laid off almost thirty percent of his employees."

"Wow. Sounds pretty serious."

"It is. And while sixty-five thousand dollars might seem small in the light of a huge company, if he's cash-strapped, he's not going to be in the mood to extend a personal loan."

Lindsey organized everything in her mind. In Vincent Lambert they had a suspect, a motivation and a possible link to the crime all wrapped up in one package. Now all they had to do was prove it.

"It seems like the perfect time to search the man's office for a link to my father—"

"Whoa." Kyle held up his hand, shaking his head adamantly. "Slow down. First of all, I'm no P.I., and even if I was, that wouldn't exactly be legal."

She frowned. He might be right, but she refused to sit around and do nothing. "So this is it? We stuff ourselves with hors d'oeuvres and dessert and then leave?"

"It could be worse." He shot her a grin. "The food is fantastic. There's romantic music in the air. I've got a beautiful woman beside me."

"Kyle."

"Seriously. Give people a couple hours of good food and alcohol, and it's amazing what you are able to pick up."

"That's a plan I can work with."

"But enough about Mr. Lambert for now." Kyle took a sip of his lemonade while gazing at her with his deep blue eyes. "We have all evening to study the man first-hand. In the meantime, I have a question that's been puzzling me for a while."

"Okay." Lindsey's stomach fluttered.

"You're single, intelligent and beautiful, but there doesn't seem to be a Romeo in your life. If there were, I'd insist you dump him because he certainly hasn't played the role of valiant hero this past week."

"A chauvinistic remark?"

"Not at all. I just think you deserve someone who will go out on a limb to ensure you're okay."

She sat back, surprised at the directness. *Always a bridesmaid, never a bride…* No. She wasn't going there again. But was he asking because he was interested, or because he felt sorry for her?

She cleared her throat. "What can I say? Romeo was always highly overrated in my opinion. The whole dying-for-love thing turns me off. One can't exactly savor bliss while dead."

Kyle laughed. "Touché. But you still didn't answer my question."

"At the moment? No. There is no Romeo, or Prince Charming, or any other fairy-tale character at my side."

*Though you, Kyle Walker, certainly could pass for a knight in shining armor.*

"Ah…at the moment." He cocked his head, eyes twinkling. "So that means there has been someone…or maybe there's someone specific you're hoping for a re-lationship with?"

She grabbed a square of cheese and stuffed it in her mouth, wondering if he could read her mind. Her thoughts were filled with far too many daydreams about him lately.

She swallowed. "I've dated a few people, but nothing ever became serious. My mom got sick, I left school, and now there's my father. I don't know. There always seems to be someone else to care for." It was time to turn the tables. Quickly. "What about you? Any woman waiting for you to return home?"

He smiled, showing off the dimple in his left cheek. "I guess I asked for that."

"You certainly didn't expect to ask me without having to answer yourself, now, did you?"

"Of course not." He wiped his mouth with a cocktail napkin, wadded it up and tossed it onto the table. "My job keeps me busy, and I admit I enjoy it, but my career has caused a bit of strain on my dating life."

"That is sad."

"I guess I've been waiting for the right woman to show up."

*Like I've been waiting for the right man.*

Lindsey stared out across the crowded patio and tried to sort out her thoughts. Women in black cocktail dresses and high heels mingled with men in tuxes. The music drifted into a soft ballad. Above her the stars were beginning to shine. The breeze was gentle. But what made the night perfect was the man sitting across from her.

What did she honestly think about Kyle Walker's unexpected entrance into her life? With all that had happened the past few days, she'd been able to avoid picturing herself in a relationship with him. But it was getting harder and harder to do.

Kyle was kind, handsome and dependable. The truth was, he was all the things she'd ever imagined in a husband.

*But the timing is all wrong.*

All wrong? Hadn't that always been her excuse? If she kept looking for the perfect time to fall in love she'd never have the chance to enjoy marriage and a family.

The very idea knocked her for a loop. She'd never thought about why she cut off relationships. It seemed right at the time. Her mother's illness, too many cases at the adoption agency, her father's prostate cancer…

So what did that make her? Lindsey Taylor. Perpetual rescuer. No time for love. Single. Being single wasn't a bad thing. She had plenty of single friends who were perfectly happy with their identities as aunts, uncles and godparents. And up to this point, she'd honestly thought she would remain in that category.

But her excuses no longer seemed valid. Had she, like Kyle, simply failed to make finding love a priority? She'd assumed that when it was the right time, love would hit like Cupid's arrow straight through the heart. But why was a relationship any different from anything else? Sometimes good opportunities came at bad times.

She'd tried not to let herself think about what she could have with Kyle, but that hadn't stopped him from showing up in her dreams.

"Lindsey?"

She glanced up, catching his grin. "Yeah?"

"You look as though you're a thousand miles away."

"I'm sorry. I..." She hesitated.

What was she supposed to tell him? That she'd started to wonder if he was the one? That she'd just realized that her heart wanted her to take a chance even though he lived a thousand miles away and a relationship between them would be hard and complicated?

She took a bite of cake. More excuses. All relationships—no matter how good—were hard.

"Lindsey. And Kyle, I believe." Vincent Lambert stepped up to their table with a drink in one hand. "I'm so glad the two of you decided to come."

Lindsey looked up at their host, trying not to choke on the piece of cheesecake in her mouth. Pricey tux...Italian shoes...expensive gold watch flashing on his arm… If the man was having financial problems, she couldn't tell by the way he dressed. She swallowed, held out her hand and smiled. It was time to play ball. "We appreciate the invitation, Mr. Lambert. It's a wonderful party."

"If it raises money for the kids, I'll be happy." He shook their hands, seemingly enjoying the social obligations of making the rounds at his party. "Is your father better?"

"He is. Thank you for asking." Lindsey fumbled with her napkin, realizing that the man made her uncomfortable. "He sends his regrets, but I'm sure he'll be in touch once he's home from the hospital."

"Please tell him I hope he feels better soon."

Lindsey glanced at Kyle. Mr. Lambert's apparent sincerity nearly erased her belief that he was involved in breaking and entering, or intimidation—nearly.

Lindsey licked her lips, nerves drying out her mouth. "I understand you have an employee by the name of Jamie McDonald?"

Mr. Lambert's brow twitched. "Jamie McDonald?"

"Do you know him?"

"Not personally, but he is on my payroll."

"I believe my father was involved in a business transaction with Jamie, and since my father is in the hospital, I need to find him. Can you help me with that?"

Taking a swig of his drink, Mr. Lambert shook his head. "I'm sorry, but I don't normally keep tabs on the personal business or whereabouts of my employees."

"I'm sorry, I just thought since you're a friend of my father's…" Lindsey struggled with what to say. "My father's in some trouble, Mr. Lambert. I'm just trying to find answers."

"I'm sorry to hear that. I'd hate for anything to happen to your father. He always was a good friend."

"Was?"

Mr. Lambert frowned. "If you'll excuse me, I need to see to my other guests. It was really great to see you again, Lindsey. Do have your father call me when he gets out of the hospital."

*I'd hate for anything to happen to your father.*

Lindsey leaned forward as Vincent Lambert walked away. "That was a threat."

"A threat?" Kyle asked.

"And he was polite. Too polite."

"Meaning?"

"I don't know." Lindsey stabbed at a strawberry with a toothpick. "I don't like him."

"You're biased," Kyle said.

"With reason."

"True," he conceded.

"Think about it. A real friend would have promised to visit or call or send flowers, but he said my father should call him. And then there was the I'd-hate-for-anything-to-happen-to-your-father comment. He knows I've figured out what's going on."

"I'll be the first to agree that there could be something behind what he said, but I'm not sure about the threat."

She stretched her back, which was already sore from wearing high heels. "I hope you're right. What now?"

"I think it's time to mingle."

An hour and a half later, they'd met the principal of Texas Liberty and learned everything there was to know about charter schools and the need for disadvantaged kids to receive a better education. They'd also met several of Vincent's employees. One in particular was more than happy to share inside information on the financial status of the company. According to this man, who'd already had too much to drink despite the relatively early hour, Lambert Enterprises was indeed in serious financial trouble.

Having exhausted their investigative powers for the evening, they said their goodbyes and headed out. Lindsey looked up at the twinkling stars, drawing in a deep breath, thankful for a moment of reprieve from the stress of the week. "It's beautiful tonight, isn't it?"

"And the company isn't bad, either."

She smiled, enjoying how comfortable she was with him. As she turned to thank him for the compliment, something caught her eye.

An orange glow flickered across the street. A man leaned against a dark blue van, smoking a cigarette. The light of the street lamp illuminated the left side of his face. Her heart froze. Long hair, a sharp nose…

It was him.

"Kyle. It's Jamie McDonald. He's watching us."

Kyle took a step toward the man. "I've had enough of this—"

Lindsey held Kyle back. "He's not worth your getting hurt."

"Who said I'm going to lose?"

"Kyle…"

He hesitated, then grabbed Lindsey's hand. "You're probably right. He's not worth it. Let's go to my car. Slowly, until he can't see us anymore."

They walked a few steps, Lindsey's heart skittering

in her chest as she forced herself not to run. Then Kyle's pace quickened and they rushed toward the car. She gasped for breath, fear burning her lungs.

*I'd hate for anything to happen to your father.* She couldn't get the words out of her head.

What had Mr. Lambert meant? That her father's life was in danger if he didn't pay up? Surely she was reading too much into the situation. But if so, then why was one of Mr. Lambert's employees still following her? Was he planning to go after her father?

Goose bumps ran up her forearms despite the balmy night air.

No. Her father was safe at the hospital. He was safer there than almost anywhere else, probably. Right?

Kyle opened the passenger door, let her in, then hurried around to the other side.

"What if they went after my father?" she asked as he slid into the seat.

Kyle started the engine and they took off down the street. "Doesn't seem likely."

"They know he has the money."

She looked in the side-view mirror to see if Jamie had followed them. A pair of headlights glared back at her. But a minute later, the vehicle turned. She kept waiting for the van to show up again, but it didn't. After a few tense minutes, she pulled out her phone, her hands still trembling. She punched in the number for the hospital. After a dozen rings, someone finally answered.

"Yes, this is Lindsey Taylor, and I'm calling to check on my father, George Taylor. I—"

"Miss Taylor?"

"Yes. Is he all right?"

"I was just about to call you."

There was a pause on the line. Lindsey felt her mouth go dry as a wave of nausea struck.

"I don't know how else to say this, Miss Taylor, but your father, he...he's disappeared."

# SIXTEEN

"My father's disappeared."

Darkness closed in on her. She flipped her phone shut and pressed her hand against her chest. Her heart raced. Her breathing quickened. If she didn't calm down, she was going to hyperventilate. The nurse said "disappeared." Not "checked out" or "been released."

"Lindsey, take a deep breath." Kyle pulled the car over and let the engine idle. "What happened?"

Her father was gone. And someone wanted his life-insurance money. In her mind, there was only one explanation. "He's kidnapped my father. Vincent Lambert and his long-haired thug."

His eyes widened. "The hospital said that?"

She hiccuped. "No…just that he was…gone." She held her breath and tried to stop the hiccups. Maybe she was jumping to conclusions. Maybe he'd simply gotten fed up with staying at the hospital and decided to leave. But without calling her? No. Whatever had happened, his leaving hadn't been of his own accord. She was sure of that.

"He couldn't have just disappeared." She caught his

confused expression in the pale light of a street lamp as he spoke. "He didn't check out?"

"No." Hiccup. "The nurses' station doesn't know where he is. And all his—" hiccup "—things are gone. His wallet. His reading glasses. His toothbrush."

Wallet…glasses…toothbrush…wait. Maybe that told them something. Jamie McDonald wasn't likely to let her father collect his personal things. Why hadn't he got a cell phone when she'd insisted last fall that he needed one for his safety? Once again, he was too stubborn.

"It sounds like he might have left on his own, Lindsey," Kyle said.

The hiccups stopped. It was possible. Wasn't it?

Kyle merged back into the traffic and took a right at the stop sign. "We'll check out your father's house to see if he's there. But I think before we talk to the police, we've got to have something more than rumors that Lambert's short on cash and might have had your father kidnapped."

"The police." She felt her throat constrict. Not that she expected they could track down and convict Lambert on their own. She had no experience in investigating a criminal case, and while Kyle had some expertise, even he'd stated that there were lines he couldn't legally cross. It was just that having to call the police— again—made her feel so desperate.

"I've already filed a report on the Internet fraud," he continued. "Though I've told you before that the chances of your father recovering all his money are slim. And if Vincent Lambert is the culprit in this situation, I have a feeling he'll be as good at covering his tracks as Abraham Omah. Although Lambert was careless with Jamie."

The odds might be against them, but her father's life was at stake in a completely different way now. Losing all his physical possessions no longer seemed so terrible in the face of his disappearance.

She took in a ragged breath and tried to focus. "So how do we go about proving Lambert's involved?"

"We've got to have some evidence to back our theory that he's short on cash and desperate for the money. Along with that, anything that might prove he'd been involved with your father, as well as any evidence of unscrupulous transactions in the past that might show he's ruthless enough to step on the other side of the law."

"Again, how?"

Kyle took her father's exit off the highway and headed toward his neighborhood. "This is really no different than compiling a due diligence report for a client. It's basically an in-depth background check."

Her panic subsided slightly. As long as they were doing something, she wouldn't feel quite as helpless. "You think we can find something?"

"That is the sixty-five-thousand-dollar question."

Kyle parked in front of her father's house. As soon as he stopped the car, she jumped out and ran up the walk, keys in hand. Dark shadows danced along the front of the house but tonight, she didn't care. Anything in the bushes better watch out.

Inside, the house looked normal. The carpet was dry, the back window had been replaced and the furniture was back in order. But a quick look down the hall revealed what she'd feared. There was no sign of her father. Sammy rubbed against her, hungry for attention.

She picked up the spoiled feline and he purred

against her cheek. The poor thing had spent almost a week on his own. A week in which she didn't feel as if they'd come any closer to the truth. If anything, their discoveries had raised more unanswerable questions.

She fed Sammy and cleaned out his litter box. Then she leaned against the edge of the bar, arms wrapped around her waist, trying to gather the energy she was going to need for the next few hours. It was already after ten o'clock, and all she felt like doing was curling up in bed and sleeping for the next few days.

Sammy devoured his dinner. At least someone was happy. There was nothing more she could do here tonight. "Are you ready to go?"

"I've been thinking." Kyle stood in front of her father's desk, hands on his hips.

"About?" she asked.

"You're not going to like this."

"Like the situation could get any worse." She bit her lip, wishing she hadn't said that.

"There is another option," Kyle said, turning toward her.

Kyle studied her expression. Did he really want to tell her this? He saw fear behind her eyes as he hesitated. If he was right, her father had a lot more to worry about than the likes of Jamie McDonald, who up to this point seemed more of a nuisance than anything else.

Ten years of working with fraud cases had taught him more than he ever wanted to know about the criminal mind. He knew how an Internet scammer thought, and

Abraham Omah's next move could be the final straw, sealing George Taylor's fate.

"Sit down for a second, Lindsey," he said.

Lindsey sat down on the edge of the couch, hands clasped in her lap, jaw clenched tight. She looked pretty in her black dress, gold heart necklace and heels—she'd been the prettiest girl at Lambert's party, in his opinion. He was done denying the attraction that had simmered between them this past week and he'd been hoping to end the evening with a kiss beneath the Texas stars. Her father going missing hadn't been a part of his plan. But once this was all over, he was going to find a moment to tell her how he felt.

Until then, finding Abraham Omah would have to remain the top priority. Her father's life depended on it.

"What is it, Kyle?" she asked.

"I could be wrong about what I'm about to say."

She held up her hand. "I want to know what we're up against. Everything that we're up against."

"Okay." He'd give it to her straight. "I'm not sure your father's disappearance has anything to do with Lambert."

Her brow furrowed. "What do you mean?"

"First of all, the man has a pretty good alibi—one hundred-plus guests mingling outside his million-dollar home. Although he could have sent Jamie to kidnap your father. But then I'd assume Jamie would be standing guard, not smoking outside the party."

"I suppose you have a point, but then who's left in the scenario?"

Kyle took a deep breath and let it out slowly. "I haven't told you everything about how these Internet scams work. In a number of cases, the victims are requested to travel to another country to pick up the cash they've been promised."

She blinked twice. "Where would they want him to go?"

"It depends on who the scammers are, where they are working from and who they've paid off. In certain cases, you'll even find that the scam artist has bribed government officials and hired actors to make the setup appear legitimate."

She shook her head. "My father would never fly halfway around the world for something like this."

"Just like he'd never sell all your mother's porcelain figures, or cash in his life insurance, or—"

"That's different."

"How is it different? We know your father trusts Omah and believes that he's going to get the money. He's invested his entire life savings in this deal—far too much to turn around and simply throw away his chance at getting the money this late in the game."

"That's just it. My father doesn't have any money left, and his credit cards are maxed out. Why would he walk out of the hospital and jump on a plane?"

"Six million dollars."

She combed her fingers through her hair. "Say he did receive an e-mail from Omah asking him to pick up the cash. He still has to pay for the ticket."

"Then there has to be another source. Can you think of anything?"

"I don't think he's been home." She glanced around the room. "He would have fed Sammy."

"Is there another friend he might have borrowed from? Or a credit card he could have used? He could have signed up for one that came in the mail. The advances are usually fairly high. Maybe one that wasn't listed in his paperwork—"

"Wait a minute."

She picked up her purse, dumping its contents on the couch. She opened her wallet and started flipping through her cards.

"Kyle…" Her voice held a note of panic.

"What is it, Lindsey?"

"My Visa card. It's gone." She fumbled through the rest of the wallet. "I can't believe he would take it. My purse was sitting beside his bed…I went into the rest-room…"

"Okay, this is good, actually. Very good." He sat beside her on the couch and put his arm around her. "Credit cards leave paper trails. Now we can track him, which means we have a better chance of finding him. I'll be right back," he said.

Within five minutes, he'd grabbed his laptop from the car and set it on the bar. He slid onto a chair in front of the screen as it buzzed to life and motioned for Lindsey to join him. He tapped his fingers against the bar—why did it take so long when every minute counted? The desktop finally appeared, and he launched the Internet browser. If her father did plan to leave the country, they needed to catch him before his flight left.

If it wasn't already too late. He'd heard horror stories of families contacted to pay ransom. The scammers' intent was to play off the vulnerability and embarrass-ment of the victim. Many of these victims had been murdered. Others were reported as missing.

But he wasn't going to let that happen to Lindsey's

father. The assignment had become personal—very personal. Losing George Taylor would be like losing Michael all over again.

He located the credit card Web site and let her type in her password. A few more clicks and they were there.

"Here it is. There was a ticket purchased today to London." He scrolled down. "And a hotel reservation for the next three nights."

Lindsey pressed the back of her hand against her mouth. "He actually walked out of that hospital, went to an Internet café then got on a plane? I…I can't believe he did this."

"Lindsey."

"I'm okay." Her breathing grew ragged. "What time does the plane leave?"

Kyle opened another window and started searching for flight times. He glanced at his watch. "The plane left at seven o'clock."

They'd missed it.


Lindsey started pacing. He'd been right—the situation could get worse. Much worse. She naively believed that her father was safe while in the hospital. She couldn't have been more wrong.

"We're going to find him, Lindsey. I've got contacts in London that will work on this for me. I even have some connections with a couple of ex-Secret Service who owe me a favor. I'll call them and get things going from that side. My tech guys have been tracing Omah's Internet protocol address from your father's computer. They've already discovered links to a 419 ring we've been trying to take down for the past nine months. That puts us ahead in the game."

"I want to know what happens now that he's there."

"Okay." Kyle propped his elbows against his knees, trying to figure out how to tell her. "More than likely he'll be met by Omah himself at the airport. By now, of course, he has your father's confidence and your dad will be glad to meet him. They'll have dinner or drinks at the hotel bar. But then your father will want to see the money."

Lindsey sat down across from him. "But there isn't any money."

"Ah, but there is. Omah will escort him somewhere. Perhaps to a room in the hotel, or more than likely, to an undisclosed location outside town. A small house or apartment. It will have a windowless room with armed guards."

"Guards?"

"Yes. And a suitcase filled with stacks of hundred-dollar bills." Kyle paused for a moment. "But there's a catch. The money will be covered in black, chalky powder."

She shook her head. "What are you talking about?"

"They'll tell your father not to worry, that it isn't uncommon for the cash to be coated to keep it from being stolen or spent."

"But it can be cleaned?"

"Of course." Kyle nodded. "Which is exactly what they'll tell your father. There'll be another man there, wearing rubber gloves and perhaps a doctor's mask, who will pour a solution into a dish and then drop the bills in to clean them."

"And does it work?"

"When he pulls them out, they look as if they've just been printed at a U.S. mint. Clean and green."

"So what's the catch?"

"They run out of cleaning solution."

"Which is expensive?"

"Very."

She felt as if she might throw up. "How much?"

"Two hundred, maybe three hundred thousand dollars."

There was no question any longer about what she had to do. She jumped up. "I'm going to London."

"Lindsey, wait. There's nothing you can do. Going to London will only put your own life in danger. These men are ruthless, and they know exactly what they are doing."

There was a catch in his voice. His eyes shifted to the ground. Lindsey froze. There was something he wasn't telling her.

"What is it, Kyle? There's more?"

"There is." He stopped. "There's often another stage to the scam."

She took in a deep breath. "Go on."

"Your father might not have any money left, but the scammers have one more trick up their sleeve." He looked her straight in the eye and reached for her hand. "They hold him for ransom."

# SEVENTEEN

Lindsey started shoving her things back inside her purse. "I'm going to London."

"Wait." Kyle gripped her shoulders, but she jerked away. "I'm serious, Lindsey. You can't reason with these people. They're criminals, and they won't stop until they get what they want."

"My father doesn't have anything left to give them." Her shoulders slumped. "How can they demand something that's not there?"

"They go after the family's money. Stripping a person of everything doesn't faze them." His jaw tightened. "Neither does murder."

"Murder? Don't tell me that, Kyle."

"Trust me. I'd rather be telling you anything else at this moment."

How had this gone from answering a simple e-mail request—fraudulent as it was—to a possible ransom, or…or murder? She pressed her purse against her stomach as nausea took over again.

He gently pulled her onto the couch beside him. "They know your father is in a vulnerable state of mind, and they won't think twice about taking advantage of him."

His words only reinforced her resolve. "Which is exactly why I'm taking the next flight to London. We have his hotel information. It won't be hard to find him."

*Unless the scam had already turned far more deadly.*

No. She fought the nausea. Kyle had no proof that her father was being held for ransom. For all they knew, his original scenario was correct. They'd show her father the suitcase with the dirty money, and he'd convince them that he didn't have another dime to his name. And that would be the end of Abraham Omah. It had to be. They'd already drained her father of everything he had. There was nothing left for them to take.

*Except his life.*

She shuddered, knowing Omah wasn't the only threat to her father's life.

"What if he has another stroke?" she asked, playing with the heart-shaped locket on her necklace. "You've seen what stress does to him. If he has another stroke, he has three hours to get to a hospital to prevent any permanent disabilities, according to his doctor. And do you think some crazed con man is going to take him to a hospital?"

He shook his head. "Lindsey, you're jumping to conclusions."

"Jumping to conclusions?" Her voice cracked as it rose in volume. "Any minute now I could receive a phone call demanding money if I ever want to see my father again. This situation is so out of control that anything could happen!"

"I was just trying to give it to you straight, Lindsey. I'm sorry."

She strode toward the window overlooking the backyard. Anger she'd allowed to simmer began to boil. She clenched her fists against her sides. Tears welled in her eyes. Light from the porch lit up her father's begonias and hibiscus that had wilted in the afternoon heat. How many evenings had she sat on the back porch drinking iced tea and reading a book while her father tended to his flowers? Would he ever get the chance to work in his garden again?

No matter how hard she tried, she still couldn't wrap her mind around all this. Facing a possible ransom was completely daunting. What kind of person did something like this to another human being?

Lindsey spun back around and caught Kyle's expression. None of this was his fault. And he certainly didn't deserve to be yelled at. Especially since he understood exactly how she felt.

"I'm sorry." She sat back down beside him. "I know I need to be aware of what I'm up against."

He reached and touched her cheek. "I just wish I could fix all this for you, but I can't."

"You've done way more than your share." She caught his hand and pressed it against her face for a moment. "But I have to go. I've got to find my father."

"The next available flight won't be until morning. We can book seats online right now if you want."

*Seats. He was coming with her.*

She smiled and he pulled her into his arms. She melted against his chest, his heartbeat steady against her ear.

Yeah, she'd fallen for him all right. Hook, line and sinker.

"Thank you," she whispered.

"You're welcome."

She looked into his eyes, wishing she could tell him how she felt. But she'd have to leave that for another day, when her world didn't feel as if it was about to fall off its axis.

He brushed a strand of hair away from her face. "The best thing you can do for your father right now is get a good night's sleep—"

"I can't," she protested.

"Arriving in London exhausted won't help your father. We can arrange for your dad's neighbor to take care of Sammy, then we'll stop by your apartment for your passport and whatever else you need. After that, we'll go to my sister's. I'll sleep on the couch and we can leave early in the morning."

"Are you sure about this?"

"I'm sure I'm not letting you go alone."

An hour and a half later, Kyle parked in his sister's driveway. The place was dark except for the outside lights and a bluish glow radiating from the television. Kerrie had told him not to worry about what time they got in— she understood exactly what Lindsey was going through.

He shut off the engine, unlocked the car and grabbed Lindsey's suitcase from the backseat, hoping he'd remembered everything. Despite the late booking, he'd managed to secure two seats on a flight out of Dallas at 6:00 a.m. with a connection in Chicago. They would arrive in London at six-thirty Saturday morning. A whole eighteen hours behind her father.

He followed Lindsey up the walk. She'd said little

on the drive over—he knew it was killing her that the earliest flight was still six hours away.

The truth was, no matter how much Kyle wanted to help—no matter how much experience he had in dealing with fraud cases—there were limits to what he could do in many situations.

He was afraid this was one of those situations.

*God, I need a miracle.*

His sister met them at the door, a book in one hand, the remote in the other. She was the only person he knew who could read with the television on.

"I'm sorry it's so late," Kyle said, dropping their bags in the hallway.

"I told you not to worry." Kerrie shoved a wayward strand of hair behind her ear. "Though if you ever move back to Dallas, I might make you a spare key."

He glanced at Lindsey before she turned away from him. "Now, *that's* an interesting idea."

Kerrie shut off the television, dropping the remote on the couch. "Do you have everything you need?" she asked, eyeing his compact bag.

"I think so." After ten years of international travel, one thing he had learned to do was pack a carry-on filled with the basics. Traveling light simplified the stress of airport travel.

"I'm fine." Lindsey's normally perky smile didn't reach her eyes.

Kerrie yawned. "I won't promise to be up when the two of you leave, but there's yogurt and fruit in the fridge, and I've set the coffeemaker for four."

A whole four hours to sleep. And he wasn't done working yet.

"You're an angel." He leaned over and kissed her on the cheek. "Good night, sis."

"Thanks, Kerrie," Lindsey added.

She started down the hall with her book tucked under her arm. Lindsey started after her to the guest room, carrying her bag.

"Lindsey?"

"Yeah?" She turned to face him.

Her eyes were red from crying, but the fear had vanished. He looked at her for a moment, wondering if he should have tried harder to talk her out of going. The problem was, if he'd known this much about Michael's situation, nothing would have stopped him from jumping on a plane. He understood exactly why she was going.

But if anything happened to her father…or to Lindsey…

"It's going to be all right."

"You can't promise me that."

"No, but I can promise that I'll do everything in my power to make sure your father comes out of this okay. I'm not losing anyone else to these guys."

She pressed her lips together and nodded.

"And when this is over…" There were so many things he wanted to say. So many things he wanted to fix. If determination counted for anything, he'd have Abraham Omah in a jail cell by tomorrow night. "We'll find your father."

"I know." She blinked back tears, exhaustion written on her face.

Why was he being such a coward? It wasn't a great time to tell her, but it was now or never. Do it, he commanded himself.

"What I really wanted to say was that, when this is over, I'd like to find a way to keep seeing you."

"I…I'd like that."

The house was quiet. He grasped her hands and heard his heart. For a moment, everything seemed to slip away. Lindsey had awakened something real inside him and he wasn't going to let her go again. No matter what the future held.

He leaned forward until he could feel her breath on his face. She smiled as he moved in—

"Uncle Kyle?"

His attention snapped toward the hallway. The nightlight revealed Caileigh, standing on the threshold of the living room, her hair messy from sleep, wearing pink pajamas with fairies dancing on the front.

He squeezed Lindsey's hands before letting go. The moment was gone. For now.

He knelt down and Caileigh ran into his arms. "Hey, sugar. I missed you today."

She gave him a hug, then stood back, arms folded across her chest. "Are you going to marry Miss Lindsey?"

Kyle stood up. "Miss Lindsey and I have been friends for a very long time, and right now I'm helping her find her father," he stammered.

The little girl quirked a brow, looking far too grown up for six. "You didn't answer my question, Uncle Kyle."

Lindsey cleared her throat and smiled. "Would you mind if I tucked you in? I never had a little sister to read good-night stories to."

Caileigh's attention shifted. "You'll read me a story? Even though I'm not supposed to be out of bed?"

The promise of a story was the perfect distraction.

Caileigh reached up and took Lindsey's hand. "Will you read 'Five Flying Fairies'? It's my favorite."

"Then 'Five Flying Fairies' it is."

Kyle resisted the urge to kiss Lindsey in front of his niece. "Get some sleep. I'll see you in the morning," he said, winking at her.

He watched Lindsey walk down the hall holding his niece's hand.

*If she's the one, Lord, help me work out the details. And help us find her father before it's too late.*

He glanced at his watch.

It was early in London, but not too early to make a few calls and ask for a few favors.

Lindsey picked at the piece of grilled chicken with her plastic fork and frowned. After one layover and another flight, her stomach churned as if she'd just gotten off a roller-coaster ride. Eating was the last thing she wanted to do.

It was already midnight in London, which meant her father had landed twelve hours ago.

*Do not lose heart.*

She squirmed at the reminder, realizing she'd done exactly that. The helplessness of being half a world away was driving her crazy. Wishing the plane would suddenly accelerate into warp speed didn't help.

*Don't lose heart.*

"Okay, God. I get it."

"Get what?" Kyle looked up from his book. Apparently the past twenty-four hours had done nothing to his appetite. He'd already wiped out the chicken, salad, roll and slice of cake.

"Sorry. I have a bad habit of mumbling to myself."

"Ever get any good feedback, or maybe some good advice?"

"Very funny." She dropped the fork onto the tray and crossed her arms—there was no use even trying to eat. "You know, I've really tried to do what we talked about in church on Sunday. To keep my eyes focused on what is unseen. To remember that this world is temporary and along with it, all our troubles. I thought as long as my father was all right, it didn't matter that he'd lost his life savings. But everything is different now."

The flight attendant stopped beside their seats and took their trays. Kyle popped open his soda.

"One thing I learned from Michael's death is that I couldn't put conditions on God's promises."

She snapped her tray table back into place. "Meaning?"

"Michael always struggled emotionally, but I remember thinking that as long as nothing devastating ever happened to him, he'd be okay. Then Michael met Anya and everything fell apart. After he died, I almost walked away from God. I was so angry over what I'd lost."

"What stopped you?"

"God pumped some sense back into me and made me realize that I have to trust Him no matter what. Sin was never in His plan, but He can work things together for good."

"Even in losing Michael?"

"It was the toughest thing I ever faced, but yes." He flipped his book over and set it in his lap. "Since Michael's death, I've been able to help dozens of people who have fallen for various scams. None of it will ever take away the hurt or regret over his death, but it does make me feel as if something good has come from it."

"I don't know if I can do that." She bit her lower lip. "I mean, I trust God and understand that there are consequences to sin, but when those consequences affect others, it's just not fair."

"No, it's not."

"What about Anya? You can't tell me that you've forgotten about her. Michael had a choice, but in reality, she was responsible."

He combed his fingers through his hair. "That's why I'm so determined to bring down as many of these scammers as I can. Stopping them from victimizing someone else is my way of getting back at Anya."

Lindsey sighed. "It's just so hard."

"It is."

Feeling restless, she reached for the phone on the back of the seat in front of her and studied the directions. "I'm going to check my messages. Maybe my father has called."

The first message was from Sarah, who was back from her honeymoon. The second was from someone selling time-shares in Vegas. She almost laughed at the irony. The last message was from her father.

"Lindsey, this is Dad. I'm calling from London, and…" There was a crackling sound. "I'm sorry, Lindsey. Maybe Uncle Lewis might be able to help."

Someone else came on the line. "We're holding your father, Miss Taylor. You've got forty-eight hours to wire one hundred thousand dollars."

# EIGHTEEN

"What's wrong?" Kyle asked as he watched the color drain out of Lindsey's face.

"You were right," she said, putting the phone back with trembling hands. "They're holding my father for ransom. He spoke for a moment, then someone else came on—someone with a strong English accent—and demanded money."

Kyle wanted to slam his fist into the seat in front of him. He'd prayed this wouldn't happen. "How much do they want?"

"A hundred thousand dollars." She grabbed the air-sickness bag and scribbled the details of the demand. "Might as well be a million. I can't access that kind of money in forty-eight hours." She glanced at her watch. "Forty-two hours now."

"He knows about the life-insurance money and thinks he can play ball for more."

Kyle knew the amount seemed astronomical, but he'd seen this scenario play out before. It had amazed him how quickly family members had managed to pull the sum together. And Omah knew it. The amount was large enough to fatten the crook's pocketbook, but small enough to make it possible for a desperate family to scrape it together. Omah also knew Lindsey would have her own set of credit cards to max out and a whole other set of friends to borrow from. He was determined to get every dime he could.

And when he was done?

Kyle's jaw tensed. He knew all too well the odds of Mr. Taylor getting out of this alive.

Kyle angled the bag where she'd written out the message, trying to decipher her handwriting. "Who's Lewis?"

"Lewis?" She angrily wiped away a tear with the back of her hand. "He's my father's uncle, but he's been dead for fifteen years."

"Maybe he gave your father something of value that he's kept all these years."

Her laugh was raspy. "The only thing my father has from my uncle is a package of cigars from twenty-odd years ago. They were never close."

"How much are the cigars worth?"

"A couple hundred dollars, if that much."

Kyle tried to stretch out his legs in front of him. The cramped quarters of economy class weren't made for his six-foot-one frame.

Lindsey dug through her purse looking for gum or a mint—something to erase the dryness in her mouth that always came with a roiling stomach. "What do we do now?"

There had to be something they were missing. "Think hard. Your father might have been trying to tell

you something. A savings bond…a valuable painting…
a family heirloom…"

"But there isn't anything." She dropped her purse to
her lap, her search fruitless. "Even if he did have something of value from Uncle Lewis, he would have sold
that before getting rid of Mom's figurines."

He could tell they were both tired of all the dead
ends. "Are you sure that's what your father said?"

"Positive."

The Fasten Seat Belt sign came on as the plane
lurched slightly. Kyle checked to ensure his belt was
snug. "People don't always make sense when they're
under stress, Lindsey."

"The fact that he's under all this stress worries me.
He sounded confused. If he's had another stroke—"

"Don't." He clasped her hand, lacing their fingers
together. "We're going to get through this. *He's* going
to get through this."

"I didn't think it would really happen. I thought my
father would convince Mr. Omah that there was no
more money left and then Omah would let him go."

Kyle sighed as Lindsey turned away from him and
stared into the sea of darkness that surrounded the plane.
Across this vast ocean, Lindsey's father was a prisoner.
And at the moment, there was nothing either of them
could do. Waiting, Kyle thought, was a form of torture.

His heart ached for her—she looked so defeated, so
hopeless. "I'm sorry, Lindsey. I know how hard this is."

She looked up at him, her lashes wet with tears. "I
just don't know what I'll do if I lose my dad. He's the
only family I have left."

He squeezed her hand. "At least we know what we're

up against. And they don't know we're coming," he
added. "That's to our advantage."

"What good is the advantage of surprise when we
don't even know where they're holding him? Chances
are they're not going to keep him in his hotel room if
they've kidnapped him. Right?"

"Probably."

So much for trying to be positive. He ran his fingers
through his hair. He was really out of his element now.
His expertise was securities and due diligence, not
ransom. He'd only been involved in two similar cases
in the past five years. Both times, the local authorities
had stepped in and taken over. And both times, despite
the law's best efforts, the two victims involved in the
cases had been found dead.

Kyle eyed the phone in front of him. He needed to
notify his contact in London about the ransom demand.
They still had forty-two hours to come up with something. Not a lot of time, but if they worked fast and
caught enough breaks, they just might get Mr. Taylor out
alive.

"I've got about seven thousand dollars in savings I
can withdraw, and a couple of credit cards," Lindsey
said. "Sarah's parents might be able to loan me the
rest."

"I can probably come up with five or ten thousand—"

"Not unless there's no other way, Kyle. You've done
enough already."

"If you need it, I'll get it for you."

She nodded and offered him a weak smile. "I know."

"I'll notify the lead investigator on the case about the
ransom, and I'll have someone stop by the hotel and

check your father's room," he said, picking up the phone. It wasn't much, but it was a start. "It will save us time, knowing for sure whether he's there or not."

"And if he isn't?" Her eyes pleaded with him for answers.

"I don't know, Lindsey. I just don't know."

The plane shook beneath them, Kyle talked on the phone beside her, and an infant cried three rows in front of them. Lindsey felt numb. She kept waiting to wake up from the nightmare that had haunted her for the past week.

*God, I want to see my father again.*

She wanted to ask God why, to demand to know how He could have allowed this to happen. Instead, she stared out across the black expanse surrounding the airplane, feeling small and vulnerable. The only thing visible beyond the darkness was yellow rays of light on the horizon.

*The heavens proclaim the glory of God, the skies proclaim His handiwork.*

The words of the psalmist resonated deep within her. She couldn't deny it. No matter what happened, God was still in control. It was the only thing she had left to hold on to. There were no other options. No middle ground. If she'd learned nothing else this week, it was that she couldn't do this on her own.

Kyle hung up the phone beside her. "We've got some news."

"What is it?" She hoped she was ready for the next round.

"Omah's getting lazy. We were able to trace the call from the kidnappers to a rented house in south London.

We've also managed to locate several beneficiaries of your father's money. They tie in to the ring we've been tracking. This might be what we want, Lindsey."

"Are they going to the house?"

Kyle nodded. "As soon as they can set things up."

"I want to be there."

"I figured that. I've got a driver meeting us at the airport, but I had to promise we'd stay out of the way. These guys are big time, and they are not going down quietly."

Kyle sat beside Lindsey in the backseat of a silver sedan. At eight in the morning, traffic crawled and progress was slow. Two employees from his company sat up front, Daniel Rodgers at the wheel, Marcus Dodson sitting shotgun. Both were former Secret Service and some of the best employees he'd hired.

If all went according to plan, they'd not only find her father but take down a kingpin connected to over a million dollars in fraud that more than likely supported heroin trafficking across Europe. Kyle wasn't the only one wanting to bring this organization down, which gave them another advantage. They were going to get this guy one way or another.

The authorities had traced the benefactors of George Taylor's transactions to more than two dozen properties on the outskirts of London, but they didn't have the resources—or the time—to check them all before the deadline ran out. Lindsey had made some calls before landing, but collecting one hundred thousand dollars was going to take time. There was no way around it. They had to get it right the first time.

Lindsey's hand brushed against his and goose bumps surged across his forearm. He glanced up and studied her profile. Lost in thought, she fiddled with a broken nail. She was so beautiful it took his breath away. Yes, when all this was over, he was going to sweep her off her feet.

He cleared his throat and pulled out the map he'd brought. "Do you want to see where we're headed?"

She nodded.

"The city's divided into thirty-two boroughs. We're headed to this one," he said, pointing. "If all goes well, your father will be eating dinner with us tonight."

His cell phone rang. It was Charles, another inside source, high up in British national security, who'd provided valuable information throughout the years. Charles and his uncanny ability to trace the untraceable was part of the reason they were so close to taking down these guys.

"Where are you?" Charles asked.

Kyle glanced outside at the familiar, busy streets. He'd spent two years living in this neighborhood before moving back to Washington, D.C. "Fifteen minutes away at best. Traffic's slower than normal."

"No, it's not. You've just forgotten the grind."

Kyle chuckled. "How long till you make your move?"

"The team is getting set up right now. There appears to be at least two people in the house. We want to make sure nothing goes wrong."

"Nothing better go wrong. I want Mr. Taylor out alive."

"Don't worry. We all do."

Lindsey looked up at him as he spoke. Too much was riding on this. The sooner it was over, the better.

"Do you have an ambulance there?" Kyle asked.

"Lindsey's father walked out of the hospital in Dallas and straight onto a plane. It's possible he's experienced another stroke."

"They can be here within two minutes. We've got our own medic on the ground if we need him."

"Great. Call me when the team moves if I'm not already there."

"You got it."

Lindsey felt a rush of adrenaline as the car squealed to a halt a block away from where five marked vehicles were parked. Kyle had told her they'd have to stay in the car, but she wasn't sure she could do that. Her hand gripped the door handle as she strained to see down the quiet neighborhood street that had been blocked off at both ends.

A row of narrow, one-story houses lay before them. A hedge blocked part of her view, but she could still see a half-dozen officers surrounding the place. She caught sight of the butt of a weapon and shuddered. If her father was caught in a cross fire…

*Please, God. Don't let anything go wrong.*

"They've got someone." Kyle pointed as he peered through the binoculars Daniel had handed him.

She strained to see. "Let me look."

He gave them to her. The police were leading a hand-cuffed man away from the house toward a squad car. Balding, thick glasses, reddish hair… Abraham Omah? She scanned the front yard. Another officer followed carrying a computer screen. A moment later, more office equipment was carried out, and then another man in his late thirties emerged in handcuffs.

Where was her dad?

"I can't see him, Kyle."

Kyle's cell phone rang again. "Yeah?"

A moment later, he popped open his door. "The scene's secure, Lindsey. We can go. Just stay back from the house." Lindsey was out of the car and down the sidewalk before Kyle's feet hit the ground. He had to run to catch up with her. Daniel and Marcus followed them.

She scanned the property. Computer equipment filled the driveway and men in uniform stalked the perimeter, but her father was nowhere in sight.

"What's going on, Kyle?" She didn't even try to curb the panic in her voice. "My father's not here."

"Lindsey." Kyle grasped her elbow at the edge of the property and motioned for her to stop. "This is as far as we can go."

"But my father…"

A man in his late forties joined them and shook Kyle's hand.

"Charles, this is Lindsey Taylor," Kyle said. He wrapped his arm around her and pulled her close to his side. "Charles is an old friend who has led part of this investigation." Kyle turned back to Charles. "Where's her father?"

Charles glanced at Kyle and then back at her. Her stomach lurched. Something was wrong.

"I'm sorry, Miss Taylor." Charles said in a clipped British accent, rubbing the back of his head. "We've searched the entire premises. Your father isn't here."

# NINETEEN

Lindsey pulled away from Kyle and ran toward the house. Her feet pounded against the hard pavement. Her father had to be there. Somehow they'd missed him, but he was there, waiting for her. She stumbled over a rock but kept running, cutting across a patch of grass toward the driveway.

She stopped short of crashing into a uniformed officer, his hand on his holster.

Her breath caught. "My father's in there."

The man's grip tightened on his weapon. He obviously had no plans to let her by.

"Lindsey?"

She turned to Kyle. "He's in there, Kyle. He has to be."

"I'm sorry, ma'am." Charles stepped forward. "You can't enter the house, but I can assure you that your father's not in there."

She shook her head in defeat, fighting back the tears. "Then where is he?"

"We're doing everything we can to find him."

She looked at the office equipment sitting on the

driveway. They'd caught their ring of scammers, and no doubt the answers to the rest of their questions lay in the confiscated computers.

"We don't know his real name, but Abraham Omah, the man who scammed your father, is still at large. Our unit plans to do whatever it takes to bring him into custody."

"And my father?" she demanded.

"We'll do everything to find him as well," Charles promised.

Lindsey weighed her options, which were few. Forcing her way into the house would only get her arrested. She had to trust Charles, trust that he had the resources to find her father before it was too late.

She blinked away the tears.

"The best thing for you to do, ma'am, is stay out of the way while my men and I take this evidence and see if we can find anything that will help us locate your father."

She was worried that they weren't moving quickly enough. They'd spent months tracking down this ring and this sting was only the tip of the iceberg. Taking time wouldn't hurt their investigation—it would strengthen it. But she could lose her father in the process.

She cocked her head. "How long will that take?"

"A few days, a week. I don't know."

Panic swelled again. "My father has less than thirty-five hours to live."

"Lindsey." Kyle touched her arm. "He's right. We can't just go off chasing shadows."

"And I can't sit around and do nothing while some maniac murders my father!"

Kyle shook his head. "Then let them do their job."

She turned away and headed back to the car with Kyle following her. She was furious—at her father for dragging her into this situation, and at herself for not being able to find him. "You said he would be here, Kyle." She needed to blame someone, and Kyle was the closest target at the moment.

"We hoped he'd be here. I never made any guarantees. I couldn't. You know that."

She stopped beside the car, her arms pressed tightly around her waist. "Again, I'm sorry. I don't mean to take this out on you. I just don't know what do to. We've got to get this guy, Kyle."

He quirked an eyebrow. "So you're not giving up?"

"Never."

"Then let's go to your father's hotel room—Daniel got a key from the hotel manager. Maybe your father left something there that will help us figure out where he is."

Lindsey glanced at her watch. Time was running out.

Kyle pulled an empty brown suitcase out of the closet and checked the pockets for anything her father might have forgotten to unpack. So far they'd found nothing of interest. The top drawer of the dresser was filled with socks, underwear and a couple of T-shirts. His toothbrush sat on the bathroom counter beside a tube of toothpaste. A black toiletry bag hung on the back of the door. Everything was neat—there were no signs of a struggle. It was as if he'd walked out of here expecting to return.

Kyle glanced up at Lindsey, who was methodically going through a briefcase. "Anything?"

"Nothing that seems out of the ordinary. His Bible, a copy of *The Hobbit* and some travel documents." She shrugged.

It was hard to find something when you weren't even sure what you were looking for. Kyle rubbed his chin. They had to be missing something.

The concierge told him that Mr. Taylor had been dropped off at the hotel by a private car, which meant that Omah had sent someone to pick him up. It also meant Omah had still been playing the role of friend and confidante at that point.

Kyle looked through the sliding glass door that led to a small balcony. This side of the hotel overlooked half a dozen bars and restaurants that were preparing for the lunch crowd. Omah would have taken Mr. Taylor out for a few drinks and then to the undisclosed location to show him the suitcase full of dirty money. When Lindsey's father said he didn't have any more money to pay for the cleaning products, things would have turned ugly.

He doubted there would have been any question left in Mr. Taylor's mind at that point about Omah's innocence. The con man's switch from friend to foe would have been quick and shocking. Mr. Taylor would definitely know the truth by now.

Kyle pulled open the sliding door and went out to the private balcony. It was a nine-by-six area with a wrought-iron table, an umbrella and four chairs. A pen sat on the table.

Kyle looked closely at the pen—it was from a health club in Dallas. It was the only evidence he could see that Mr. Taylor had come out here.

Lindsey stepped out onto the balcony. "Anything?"

"Your dad's pen." He handed it to her, wondering what her father had been writing.

A gust of wind sent a chill down his spine despite the sunny, humid day. There was nothing more to see out here. He turned to go inside and something caught his attention—a piece of paper fluttering against the edge of the balcony. He bent down to pick it up.

"What is it, Kyle?"

He handed her a piece of hotel stationery with a few lines written neatly in black ink. "Looks like a letter your father started. To you."

Lindsey scanned the few lines of the unfinished letter, feeling her heart break. She stepped back inside the hotel room. Kyle closed the sliding door, muting the noise from outside.

"What does it say?" Kyle asked.

She cleared her throat. "'All I can do, Lindsey, is ask for your forgiveness for what I've put you through. If anything goes wrong today, I want you to know that I love you. And I need you to forgive me, even if you never understand why I did this.

"'There are so many things I never told you because I wanted to protect you and your mother. I loved her so much. I loved you both. And now…'"

"Is that it?"

"That's all he wrote." She ran her hand across the page and shook her head. "Someone must have interrupted him. He was scared, Kyle. He believed there was a chance he'd never see me again."

"I'm so sorry, Lindsey." Kyle wrapped her in his

arms and held her tight. "Omah must have arrived, stopping him from finishing the letter."

"But what did he want to tell me?" Rage suddenly gripped her and she wanted to rip up the letter. She pulled away from Kyle's embrace. This could have been avoided.

She threw down the letter and grabbed the map of London Kyle had left on the table, jabbing her finger at the center of the city. "This is crazy. He could be right next door or fifty miles away."

"Charles and his team are working as fast as they can."

"What if it's not fast enough?" Less than thirty-two hours, and her hands were tied. She could hardly stand it.

She stared at the map, looking at all the unfamiliar places and names, feeling very far away from home. Hackney, Camden, Brent, Lewisham.

Lewisham. Uncle Lewis.

"Kyle, look at this. The borough of Lewisham," she said, pointing on the map.

"What about it?"

Her breath caught in her throat and she could hardly get the words out. "I don't think my father was talking about Uncle Lewis, Kyle. I think he was trying to tell me where he is."

Kyle punched Charles's number into his cell. It was a long shot, but if Lindsey's theory was right, and the borough corresponded with one of the locations they'd already identified, they had a very real chance of finding her father.

"Charles, this is Kyle." Traffic roared in the background, but the connection was clear. "I think we might have a lead on George Taylor."

"What have you got?"

Kyle relayed the details of the cell-phone message, and the fact that Lindsey's uncle had died a decade and a half ago.

"That is odd," Charles said. "But fear can make people do and say a lot of strange things."

"Or maybe her father was trying to pass a message to her." Kyle glanced at Lindsey who was barely holding it together. He had to get the man to listen. "It makes sense, Charles. Mr. Taylor knew Lindsey would figure it out."

"Lewisham isn't much to go on, Kyle."

"It is if you can match it to one of the assets you've identified."

"Give me a second to find out what we've got on this end." Thirty seconds later, Charles came back on the line again. "Okay, I've got one location in Lewisham. A small restaurant that's been open about two years."

"The perfect setup for laundering money."

"Yes, but that doesn't mean Mr. Taylor's being held there. And even if he was in that area when he called, they could have moved him during the past twelve hours. The chances are slim, and you know that."

"Time's running out, Charles. What other leads do you have?"

"Our guys are working on the computers they confiscated earlier today, but at the moment, I'll admit this is the only possible lead we have."

"You could have Abraham Omah in custody before the end of the day," Kyle said.

Charles was silent for a moment. Then he relayed the restaurant's address. "Meet us there in an hour?"

"We'll be there."

"And stay out of the way this time."

Kyle smiled. "No problem."

Lindsey leaned against the window of the silver sedan, feeling a strong sense of déjà vu. Another location. Another possible bust. Charles's team had gone inside the restaurant, but so far, no one had emerged. And there was still no sign of her father.

She scanned the narrow roadway with the binoculars. Cars, buses and bikes filled the busy street that was home to about a dozen shops and restaurants, and a high-rise of flats. A woman pushed a stroller past an Asian restaurant. Another woman ran by in a Windbreaker, listening to an iPod. A man chatted with someone standing inside a doorway.

She zoomed in on the targeted restaurant. Two cars were parked in front and a third in the alley that ran along the side of the shop. Beyond that car was a Dumpster.

Charles emerged from the restaurant. He stared down the street, his phone to his ear.

Kyle's cell rang.

"He's not here, Kyle. I've got two waitresses and a cook who speaks a little English. Unless you want to order lunch, this is a dead end."

She searched the street again with the binoculars, and zoomed back to the man in the doorway. The signature *T* on a Texas Rangers baseball hat caught her eye. Lindsey squinted in the sunlight. The second man had emerged from the shadows. Her heart pounded. It was her father.

Lindsey threw the binoculars down and struggled to

unlock the door, but she couldn't seem to make her hands work the way she wanted them to.

"What is it, Lindsey? Where are you going?"

"My father. He's headed inside that apartment building." She shoved open the door and started off down the street.

"Lindsey, wait!"

Kyle jumped out of the car and hollered at Charles. She could hear Kyle and Daniel running behind her, but she wasn't waiting. Dodging an older woman pushing a shopping cart, she dashed toward the building. Fatigue from the last week was replaced by pure adrenaline. She caught the door before it shut and saw her father and the man turn the corner at the top of a staircase.

She flew up the stairs and through the doorway. "Abraham Omah!"

Her father's captor spun around, halfway down the hallway, his hand tightly gripping her father's arm. Abraham Omah looked nothing like she'd pictured. With his dark complexion and curly black hair, he could have been her next-door neighbor back home.

But his eyes were cold and hard.

She swallowed. "I want my father. Let him go."

Her father's face paled. "Lindsey, I'm so sorry."

"It's going to be all right, Daddy."

The door to the hallway slammed open behind her. She glanced back at Charles and Kyle. "Get behind us, Lindsey," Kyle said.

Two men from Charles's team approached stealthily from the other end of the hallway, behind her father. They had them surrounded.

Lindsey moved toward Kyle and Charles as Charles raised his gun. "Game's over, Abraham."

"Not quite. If you hadn't noticed, I still have a hostage." He whipped out a gun from his jacket pocket and held it to her father's head.

# TWENTY

Lindsey's fingernails dug into the palms of her hands. *Please, God. Don't let it end this way. Please.*

Charles took another step forward. "There's no need for this to turn ugly. Let Mr. Taylor go."

Abraham pressed the gun hard against her father's temple.

Her pulse accelerated. She didn't want to find out how the Internet scammer handled face-to-face confrontations.

For a full five seconds, no one moved.

Suddenly the apartment door beside Abraham swung open. A man in a baseball cap stepped into the hall and gasped as a gun was pointed in his face. "Garki! What the—"

"Put your hands on your head!" Charles shouted as Lindsey's father collapsed.

Charles's men didn't give either suspect time to recover from the distraction. In a matter of seconds, Abraham was surrounded, patted down and handcuffed. The second man lay prostrate on the floor beside him.

Lindsey ran to her father who was slumped against the wall. "He needs an ambulance."

"I'm on it," Charles said.

"I'm okay, Lindsey," her father said as she embraced him.

"No, you're not." Relief swelled into anger. "You never should have left the hospital, and now this—"

"I'm sorry, Lindsey." Her anger quickly dissipated as tears spilled down her father's face.

Charles flipped his cell phone shut. "An ambulance is on its way. I'll meet you at the hospital when I'm done here. I'm going to need to talk to your father."

"Of course." Lindsey squeezed her eyes shut for a moment, suddenly unable to focus. The floor swayed beneath her. She braced herself against the wall.

Kyle grasped her elbow. "Are you okay?"

She shook her head, her breathing growing shallow as nausea engulfed her.

She glanced down the hall at the man who'd tried to ruin her father's life. Abraham Omah, Garki, or whatever his real name was, was being led away, his head down, gaze on the floor. Bile rose, burning her throat. She wanted him to know what he'd done, to make him understand the cruelty of his actions.

She started after him.

Kyle held her back. "Save your energy for your father, Lindsey. He needs you."

She watched Abraham Omah vanish around the corner and prayed that God would someday take away the hatred that burned in her heart for the man who'd ruined her father's life.

An hour later, Lindsey sat beside her father in a small hospital room. Color had returned to his face, his heart rate had stabilized and his blood pressure had come down slightly since the initial evaluation with the EMS team. Lindsey was still struggling with her emotions, trying to convince herself that the anger and resentment she felt didn't matter anymore because her father was okay. And as hard as it was going to be, one day they'd be able to put Abraham Omah behind them.

"The doctor says that there is no sign of a stroke." She brushed a curly lock of gray hair from her father's brow. "It's a miracle, you know."

"I might be a complete fool, but God is still good, isn't He?"

"You're not a fool, Daddy."

He wound the edge of the sheet between his fingers. "There is so much I need to tell you, Lindsey. Things about your mother...about decisions we together made before she died."

Lindsey wasn't sure she could handle any more bombshells at the moment. "You don't have to talk now. You need your rest."

"The least I owe you is an explanation. You've been through so much this past week."

"Daddy, please. You don't have to—"

"I need to."

She pressed her hands together in her lap and nodded.

"Remember how much your mother loved Christmas?" He smiled slightly at the memory.

"Yeah, Daddy."

"Your mom wanted us to spend one more holiday together before she died. She loved the lights and the Christmas music. The choir singing 'Joy to the World' and 'Away in a Manger' at church…" He closed his eyes for a moment as if he was trying to picture it clearly. "In August of that year, we found out about some experimental drugs we believed could extend her life, but insurance refused to pay for them."

Lindsey tried to grasp what her father was saying. If they'd needed money, why hadn't they told her? She'd have found a way to help defray the cost.

"I don't understand." The pulsating blare of an ambulance sounded in the distance, competing with the steady beeps of the machine monitoring her father's heart rhythm. "Why didn't I know about this?"

"Because your mother didn't want you to worry. And I…" He avoided her gaze. "I didn't want you to worry, either."

She shook her head. That simply wasn't good enough. "I dropped out of school and moved back home to take care of Mom while you worked, and you were worried that I was too young to handle things?" She held up her hand. "I'm sorry. I just… I just would have liked to have been a part of things. I thought I *was* a part of things."

"You were." He grasped her hand. "You were always the most important part of our lives."

Lindsey swallowed and took in a deep breath. "Tell me the rest."

"The experimental drugs wiped out most of our savings, but she ended up living four extra months."

Lindsey squeezed her eyes shut to stop the tears. Her mom had celebrated one last Christmas with them, just as she'd wanted.

"I would have done anything to keep her alive longer, but nothing I did was enough."

The ugly truth sunk in. He blamed himself. She'd never realized he held himself responsible for her mother's death. "You know it wasn't your fault."

He shook his head. "In trying to save her, I ended up failing you both."

"What do you mean, Daddy?"

"All I ever wanted to do was to take care of you and your mother. You two were my life. After your mother died, Abraham's letter seemed like an answer to my prayers. An easy way to pay off my debt and leave you a decent inheritance. Except Abraham kept needing money. A few hundred for bank charges, another couple thousand for customs, then another few hundred for something else…" He paused for a moment. "I kept telling myself it would be worth it in the end when I received my share of the fortune, but before I knew it I'd mortgaged the house and sold my stock options… and I still had nothing."

Lindsey's heart broke. "Because none of it was true, Daddy."

"I know that now." A solitary tear slid down her father's cheek. "Then I made another mistake by going to Vincent. And while I'd heard rumors of his unethical business activities, I thought I could trust him."

"And then his business started going under."

"He needed the cash I owed him and sent one of his men to encourage me to pay up."

"Jamie McDonald?"

Her father nodded. "Jamie's got fewer brains than a scarecrow, but he knows how to rough people up. The only way out I could think of was to cash in my life-insurance policy. I was on my way to give Jamie the money when I started feeling sick. I pulled over and walked around a bit to get some air. At some point, I must have passed out."

Abraham's promise of millions was her father's justification for everything he'd done. Borrowing money, cashing in his life insurance, taking her credit cards… Her heart ached for her father, but she grasped for a way to find forgiveness. At the moment all she could do was hold on to her faith and pray that in time they would find a way to put this behind them.

Kyle stepped into the room with Charles and cleared his throat. "How are you doing, sir?"

"They tell me I'll live."

"That's always a good sign." Kyle shoved his hands into his pockets. "You don't mind if I steal your daughter away for a couple hours, do you? She hasn't eaten all day, and I know you'd prefer she didn't end up here as well."

"She's all yours. Thank you, Kyle, and you, Charles, for everything."

Kyle nodded. "We're glad you're okay, sir."

"I'm ready to talk, Charles. I know you have many questions for me."

Lindsey squeezed her father's hand. "Are you sure, Daddy?"

"I want that felon behind bars the rest of his life."

Charles nodded. "With two more arrests and a flat full of evidence, I'd say we're on our way to doing just that."

"Thank you, Charles," Lindsey said, shaking his hand.

He smiled. "Kyle and I always have made a pretty good team. And the intel we received from you helped tremendously."

"I'm glad to hear that," Lindsey said. "And I'll continue to help in any way I can because I want you to ensure that this is the last time Abraham Omah ever has the chance to scam anyone."

Lindsey stood beside Kyle on London's famous Tower Bridge as the sun began to set over the River Thames. She'd opted for a walk before dinner, giving her time to clear her muddled mind. The breathtaking view of the waterway had helped to soothe her frayed nerves. And she loved watching cars, motorcycles and open-topped, double-decker buses zoom across the bridge, while pedestrians strolled the famed walkway.

A cool breeze tossed her hair around her face, erasing some of the effects of the warm summer day. If only it could erase the memory of the past week as well.

She leaned against the railing and glanced up at Kyle. "Is it wrong for me to hate Abraham?"

"I believe God understands—more than we realize—the immense heartache we feel at loss and betrayal."

"But I want Abraham to suffer the way he made my father suffer. The way he made all his victims suffer."

"I felt the same way when Michael died. But we're all sinners and Christ died for all of us, no matter what the sin."

"Hate the sin but not the sinner?"

"Something like that. It's hard, isn't it?

"Very."

Kyle wrapped his arm around her and drew her closer. "You just can't let your anger eat you up and destroy you."

"I guess it's just going to take time. For both me and my father."

Beside them a tourist snapped photos of the city skyline before the last light of day disappeared. A couple walked by, pushing a sleeping toddler in a stroller. Life went on. The emotional wounds would take time to heal, but she also knew that they would both one day recover from the ordeal.

Her gaze followed the path of a tour boat, white water churning at the bow, until the craft disappeared beneath the massive structure of the bridge. "You told me you had some news?"

"While you were at the hospital, I got a call from a contact in the Dallas police department. Jamie McDonald was hauled in for drunk driving and apparently, thinking he was being picked up for other, more serious crimes, tried to cut a deal with the D.A. and take Vincent Lambert down with him."

"You're kidding." Lindsey laughed. "So he verified my father's story that Jamie had been paid to get the money back?"

"That, and he gave them information about a mysterious case of fraud the D.A.'s been trying to pin on Lambert. With Jamie's cooperation, they'll have enough evidence to put the man behind bars for the next fifty years."

"That's unbelievable."

"That's what I said." He took her hands and smiled down at her. "But enough of Lambert and McDonald. You know, we never had our first date."

She smiled back, enjoying the tingling feeling that shot all the way down to her toes when he looked at her. "You don't call flying to London and tracking down a couple of bad guys a date?"

He laughed. "I was thinking more like a dinner for two at this quaint Japanese restaurant I know."

"I'll go for that."

"I was also thinking about calling up my business partner and telling him I'm moving to Dallas to work in our new offices there. You wouldn't mind, would you?"

She shook her head, unable to speak. Her heart skipped a beat or two as he leaned toward her.

"I don't want to lose you again, Lindsey."

The noisy background faded along with the busy scene until all she could see was Kyle. He brushed his lips against hers, softly at first, then deepening into a kiss full of promise and expectation.

When he pulled away, she couldn't help but grin. Perhaps her bridesmaid days were finally over.

\* \* \* \* \*

Dear Reader,

Often one of the hardest things to accept in life are the consequences of other people's mistakes. Especially when those mistakes affect our own lives. This is exactly what happened to Lindsey Taylor in FINAL DEPOSIT. Her father's decision to trust the wrong person not only wiped out his finances, but put her own life at risk.

Forgiveness isn't always easy to grant. Both Lindsey and Kyle had to choose whether or not to forgive those who had hurt them. In the end, granting forgiveness kept them from becoming bitter and ruining their own lives.

Of course, the ultimate example of forgiveness comes from God Himself. He was willing to send His own Son to die for our sins. Think about how much He loves you, and how that forgiveness sets you free from the penalty of sin.

That's amazing forgiveness. Unmerited and unearned. What an amazing expression of love.

I hope you enjoyed FINAL DEPOSIT. I love to hear from my readers. Feel free to contact me at:
contact.harris@gmail.com.
I'd also love for you to visit my Web site at:
www.lisaharriswrites.com or my blog at:
http://mbloginthe heartofafrica.blogspot.com.
There you can keep up with what's happening in my life in the heart of Africa, sign up for my newsletter and enter my frequent contests.
Blessings!
Lisa Harris

## DISCUSSION QUESTIONS

1. What was Lindsey's reaction when she found out what her father had done? Would you have reacted that way?

2. Have you ever suffered the consequences of someone else's bad decisions or choices? How did you handle it?

3. Kyle experienced the need to forgive when he lost his brother, Michael. How did he deal with anger toward Anya, the woman who scammed Michael?

4. Have you or anyone you love ever been scammed or conned? How did you or your loved one cope with it? How did it make you feel?

5. II Corinthians 4: 8-9 talks about the difficulties of life and how we will have times of despair, disappointment, hurt and anger. Have you experienced these things? When?

6. When Lindsey and Kyle are flying to London, Kyle says that one of the things he learned after Michael's death was that he couldn't put conditions on God's promises. What do you think about that idea?

7. Have you ever blamed God for something that has happened in your life?

8. Kyle says that he had to learn to trust God no matter what. He also reminds Lindsey that God can bring good out of a difficult situation for those who serve Him. Do you believe this? (Romans 8:28)

9. Can you recount a time when God has worked things together for good in your own life?

10. How did God bring about good through the situation with Lindsey's father?

11. In Corinthians 4: 16-18, Paul tells us that we shouldn't give up, because the hardships in this life won't last forever. Instead, they will help to mold us, shape us, even strengthen us to produce a glory that will outweigh everything we've gone through. Have you experienced the way hardships can make you a better, stronger person?

12. Paul says we should fix our eyes on the unseen. What does this mean to you?

13. What are some things you can do every day to fix your eyes on God?

# REQUEST YOUR FREE BOOKS!

## 2 FREE RIVETING INSPIRATIONAL NOVELS
## PLUS 2 FREE MYSTERY GIFTS

**YES!** Please send me 2 FREE Love Inspired® Suspense novels and my 2 FREE mystery gifts (gifts are worth about $10). After receiving them, if I don't wish to receive any more books, I can return the shipping statement marked "cancel". If I don't cancel, I will receive 4 brand-new novels every month and be billed just $4.24 per book in the U.S. or $4.74 per book in Canada, plus 25¢ shipping and handling per book and applicable taxes, if any*. That's a savings of over 20% off the cover price! I understand that accepting the 2 free books and gifts places me under no obligation to buy anything. I can always return a shipment and cancel at any time. Even if I never buy another book, the two free books and gifts are mine to keep forever.

123 IDN ERXX   323 IDN ERXM

| | | |
|---|---|---|
| Name | (PLEASE PRINT) | |
| Address | | Apt. # |
| City | State/Prov. | Zip/Postal Code |

Signature (if under 18, a parent or guardian must sign)

### Order online at www.LoveInspiredSuspense.com
### Or mail to Steeple Hill Reader Service:

**IN U.S.A.:** P.O. Box 1867, Buffalo, NY 14240-1867
**IN CANADA:** P.O. Box 609, Fort Erie, Ontario L2A 5X3

Not valid to current subscribers of Love Inspired Suspense books.

**Want to try two free books from another series?**
**Call 1-800-873-8635 or visit www.morefreebooks.com**

* Terms and prices subject to change without notice. N.Y. residents add applicable sales tax. Canadian residents will be charged applicable provincial taxes and GST. Offer not valid in Quebec. This offer is limited to one order per household. All orders subject to approval. Credit or debit balances in a customer's account(s) may be offset by any other outstanding balance owed by or to the customer. Please allow 4 to 6 weeks for delivery. Offer available while quantities last.

**Your Privacy:** Steeple Hill Books is committed to protecting your privacy. Our Privacy Policy is available online at www.SteepleHill.com or upon request from the Reader Service. From time to time we make our lists of customers available to reputable third parties who may have a product or service of interest to you. If you would prefer we not share your name and address, please check here. ☐

LISUS08R